*A
Harlequin
Romance*

THIS TOO
I'LL REMEMBER

by

MONS DAVESON

HARLEQUIN   BOOKS

Winnipeg • Canada   New York • New York

THIS TOO I'LL REMEMBER

First published in 1970 by Mills & Boon Limited,
17 - 19 Foley Street, London, England.

Harlequin Canadian edition published December, 1970
Harlequin U.S. edition published March, 1971

Standard Book Number: 373-51456-5.

Printed in Canada

THIS TOO I'LL REMEMBER

CHAPTER ONE

IT was sitting about in the drizzling rain that had started all this, started this journey that was ending in such a bleak and barren countryside, Deirdre thought bitterly, knowing at the same time that the blame lay entirely with herself. She shut her eyes tightly, blotting out the only signs of civilization – the never-ending telegraph poles that flashed past the train windows. From behind closed lids she thrust back the threat of tears impatiently, reminding herself for the hundredth time that a year was only a year, anyway, and that it would pass, as all things did in time.

Penetrating the stubborn barrier of aloofness with which she had surrounded herself, the sounds of closing books, suitcase catches snapping shut, impedimenta being removed from the rack, made her realize all at once that they must be nearing the end of this hateful journey. A heavy thump directly beside her brought her abruptly upright. The man who had lazed contentedly next to her all morning, partly hidden behind the sporting pages of the daily paper, was now standing in the corridor, her large case at his feet.

He smiled at her in a friendly fashion.

'I'm Bert Langton,' he introduced himself. 'I see

your luggage is labelled Limberg, and as we're nearly there I've hauled it down for you. Is this all you have?'

'Thank you, yes, except for my overnight bag here,' patting the container on the seat beside her. Sheer good manners insisted that she smile back at him, albeit a trifle perfunctorily. 'I'm Deirdre Sheldon,' she told him. 'Is this Limberg now?' she added, as buildings began to slide past the windows instead of those everlasting telegraph poles.

Langton turned sideways to glance out of the window.

'Yes, we've arrived. Not much of a place unless you happen to feel a kind of affection for it.'

There was no doubt about the affection radiating from his whole expression, and Deirdre felt amazed. As the train slowed she could see nothing to merit anything but the most lukewarm and fleeting appreciation.

Using a powder-puff sparingly and applying a light pink lipstick, she transferred her gaze to her own pale face in the mirror of her compact, and while she did so her travelling companion called good-bye, and vanished on to the railed-in platform at the end of the carriage. She watched him go with a brief sensation of dismay because he had been good enough to perform a small service for her.

Gathering up her belongings, she made her way down the swaying corridor as the train finally jerked to a halt. Right at the back of a tight little knot of passengers she stood against the rail waiting for her turn to step down out of the train, and with nothing better to do until that moment arrived she cast a glance around her to discover whether there was anything about Limberg that could warm her heart. It certainly wasn't a big station, and not in the least impressive, but she had been warned about that by Dr. Mac. But wherever she looked there were cars . . . lines of cars crowding close to the station, parked all over the place, cars of every description and vintage, their paintwork and chrome glinting in the sunshine. She told herself she would have to change her ideas of a farming community if this was their method of getting about.

Bringing her gaze back to the station, she felt it drawn by Mr. Langton and two other men, who were watching her. Bert Langton appeared to be doing all the talking while the others stood listening. She averted her eyes from the taller of these, and turned away from a contemplation that was openly appraising.

Unaccountably embarrassed, she bent to pick up her overnight bag, but Mr. Langton jumped the two high steps and took it from her, seizing her suitcase also and lowering it from the train. Then he turned to give her a hand on the steps.

'Careful now,' he said.

He introduced her to the two other men.

'This is Bill Darrell, Miss Sheldon. He's a clerk here at the railway station, and as everyone ends up here eventually he'll know if the people meeting you are anywhere near at hand.'

Wearily she looked up into the face above her, but met only kindness in the blue eyes regarding her. She told him a Mrs. Liddle was expecting her. Bill Darrell grinned at this piece of information, and replied that that was all right, then. She wasn't there yet, but her old truck would be recognizable anywhere, for it was held together by string. Indicating the man standing beside him he said to Deirdre: 'This is Blair Cameron, Miss Sheldon. He's a farmer, and as Mrs. Liddle does his tobacco, too, you'll probably be seeing more of him.'

Blair Cameron said 'How do you do' politely enough, but the expression on his face was so different from the expressions on the faces of the other two men that it quite startled her. He was tall, blue-eyed, and dark, extremely sunburned and broad-shouldered, and altogether a very personable man in his early thirties; but his eyes were the coldest she had ever seen in her life, and in addition to being cold and calculating they appeared to her to hold a derisory gleam. After subjecting her to a far from impersonal stare he appeared to become interested in another couple on the train, and Bert Langton said a regretful farewell to her, explaining that his wife would be wondering where he had got to.

'But Bill will look after you,' he told her. 'See you around, Deirdre,' and with a smile and a salute he swung away, also very tall and dark, but much more human than Blair Cameron, she was sure.

She seized the opportunity to take another long look at her new surroundings. Through the centre of the small town, cutting it quite literally in two, ran the railway line, and directly facing her was a hotel – quite a large one. And on either side of the hotel there were shops, a cinema, and a restaurant. Quite close at hand was the school, silent and deserted by comparison with the hubbub at the station, especially the two tennis-courts, but bowered in trees and pleasant enough. Everything about it suggested that it was well cared for and thoroughly well maintained, and the pupils who attended it were probably very fortunate.

Despite the warmth of the sunshine there was a cool breeze blowing round her ankles and stirring her hair, and she moved to stand more in the sunshine. She saw Bill, who had left her to enter his office, re-emerge from it and accost her quite gaily.

'Come along, Deirdre,' he said – and apparently it was to be "Deirdre" from now on – 'Blair is going to take you across to the hotel. You can lunch there and wait for Mrs. Liddle.'

'That's not necessary,' she protested, thinking that anyone could see themselves such a short distance without assistance, but her protest went unheeded. Bill took her by the arm and guided her over to the main parking-lot, and there she saw Blair

Cameron loading her luggage into the boot of a car. It was long and sleek and as grey as a battleship, and she had an impression of power . . . power that dwelt in Blair's blue eyes, and power that was almost certainly part of the performance of his car. He held open the door for her, and then slid behind the wheel. Bill looked in through the window and patted her arm, saying he was delighted to have met her, and then stepped back hurriedly as the car leapt forward.

Deirdre called through the window:

'Thank you for taking care of me, Mr. Darrell,' and the last she saw of him he was smiling and waving his hand.

There was silence in the big car as it negotiated the stretch of road which led to the crossing connecting both sides of the town. Deirdre sat close to her window and felt unable to find words for the usual small-talk.

It was the man who spoke first.

'Well, Deirdre, what do you think of our city?'

She couldn't decide whether he was simply being cynical, or whether he was deliberately mocking her. She looked at him with prim displeasure, disliking his use of her Christian name.

'I'll be able to answer that question when I've seen a little more of it.'

'There isn't much more of it. But, such as it is, we're all quite fond of it.'

'You mean you, personally, are fond of it?'

'I have a certain affection for it.' He was glancing sideways at her, his eyes bright and provocative, his manner peculiarly disturbing. Tired after her journey, and conscious that her wits were scarcely at their brightest, she wished he was more like Bill Darrell. Bill had struck her as one of the easiest people to get on with, but this man. . . . 'You don't look like a tobacco grader to me,' he told her, as they crossed the railway line and purred smoothly up to the front of the hotel. He made no effort to alight, or assist her to do so, but sat with his hands resting idly on the wheel.

'And you,' she responded tartly, 'don't look like a farmer to me.'

He laughed.

'But I assure you I am a farmer, and a good one at that. What did you expect to be come upon in Limberg? Someone in the Dad and Dave vaudeville line?' There was heavy sarcasm in his tone, and he finally made the effort and unfastened his door and walked round to hold open hers. With a wave of his hand he indicated the veranda steps. But she hung back.

'What now?' His eyebrows rose.

'My luggage. You haven't taken it out.'

'I'll get it when Mrs. Liddle comes.' His voice held a studied patience. 'There's not much point in removing it and then having to replace it if she fails to turn up and I have to run you out to her.'

'But surely it's most unlikely that she won't come—?'

'Nothing's unlikely, and all things are possible.' He took her by the arm and walked up the steps. She resented the firm grip of his fingers, and made up her mind that if Mrs. Liddle didn't turn up she would discover some means of joining her that would not involve accepting assistance from Blair Cameron ... or anyone like Blair Cameron.

'Surely I can get a taxi?' she suggested. 'Besides, I don't want to take you out of your way.'

'How do you know it would be taking me out of my way?'

'I don't, but—' She bit her lip. His irritating eyes were on her, his expression cool and amused. 'Do you mean it wouldn't be taking you out of your way?'

For answer he guided her along the length of the veranda, and through a door into the dining-room of the hotel. He seated her at a table, greeted the waitress who walked towards them with a much pleasanter smile than Deirdre had yet seen on his face, and without consulting her about her preferences ordered lunch for the two of them in affable phrases that won an answering smile for himself from the girl who accepted the order. Then he dropped into a chair facing Deirdre and belatedly inquired whether she was hungry and whether she had any particular likes or dislikes where food was concerned.

'No,' she answered.

'Good.' His smile was complacent, if not exactly approving.

The meal was eaten in near silence, her companion speaking only when it was necessary for him to attend to her needs, and Deirdre, an uneasy conviction that she was being tolerated for some reason keeping her silent in return, wished he had left her alone to buy her own lunch and wait for Mrs. Liddle. She saw Bill Darrell come in half-way through the meal, but he only smiled at her as he passed their table and ended up at one where three men were already seated.

Blair glanced at her scarcely touched plate of dessert, which she had pushed aside, and asked:

'Will you have coffee or tea, Deirdre? We mostly drink tea here, but there is coffee if you prefer it.'

She answered that she would prefer coffee.

He continued to allow his eyes to rest on her plate of dessert.

'You don't appear to have had very much appetite,' he remarked. 'Do you normally eat like a mouse?'

'Oh, not normally, but – but I haven't had very much appetite since I was ill.' Hurriedly she attempted to divert his attention, and made a remark about the tennis-courts across the road. 'Do people play much tennis here? I'm rather keen on a game myself.'

'Yes, quite a lot.' But his tone was disinterested. 'What was it you said about being ill?'

She watched him light a cigarette, and thought what an unusually shapely hand he had – for a farmer. It was tanned and strong, but the fingers were slender and his nails were beautifully cared for just as he obviously shaved himself with much precision and carefulness.

'Oh, I had pneumonia,' she answered, hoping he wasn't going to inquire what had led up to the pneumonia.

He made an observation that was just as difficult to parry.

'With all the modern drugs they have nowadays most people take pneumonia in their stride, don't they?' he said. 'But you, if you'll forgive me for saying so, look as if you failed to prove the modern rule.'

She said, almost as baldly as before:

'I had a relapse when I came out of hospital. I had to go back, and apparently they had rather a difficult time with me.'

'Good heavens!' he exclaimed. 'They must have been incredibly careless to release you in the first place.'

'I think they were probably short of beds.'

He frowned at the glowing tip of his cigarette.

'How did you manage to collect pneumonia?'

Deirdre averted her face. Even after three years she found it difficult to talk about herself and her parents' deaths, and he gathered from her expression that she was not prepared to talk.

Blair shrugged his shoulders, and apparently dismissing her affairs as quite unimportant stood up and proffered her her light hand luggage, and said crisply:

'Come along, I'll drive you out to Brand's farm where Mrs. Liddle is at present.'

They had only just reached the car, however, when he exclaimed with little or no expression:

'Why, here she is now!'

A battered utility was approaching along the road, and despite its obvious age it was travelling at great speed. Deirdre felt amazed as she studied it, and she felt still more amazed when it stopped in front of the hotel and its owner hopped out. 'Hopped' was the only way in which her impulsive movement could be described. She was dressed in blue jeans and a check shirt, and her hair was cropped so short and curled so tightly that it looked like a mat protecting her face from the sun. She wore a vividly bright lipstick, and if she hadn't done so Deirdre might have mistaken her for a man until she came from around the bonnet of the truck.

She briskly shook hands with the young girl, saying, 'I'm Mrs. Liddle, as I expect you've already guessed. Henry told me Blair had taken you in tow. How are you, my dear?' Her face seemed to fall somewhat as she looked Deirdre over. 'Dr. McIntyre said you'd been ill, but you look to me as if you're still far from well. I don't know whether you'll be able to make out with us. We're working short-handed, you know, and I was hoping you'd be able to pull your weight.'

The words were hurried, as if she had little time for polite conversation, and their implication caused Deirdre's heart to sink. She said hurriedly that she was quite sure she'd be able to manage, and she wasn't really as fragile as she looked. Besides, she enjoyed working hard.

'I'll manage,' she repeated. 'I really will! I'm getting much stronger every day, and I promise I won't let you down. I may not be expert at first, as I have never graded before, but Dr. McIntyre said anyone could grade if they'd a reasonable amount of sense.'

Mrs. Liddle snorted, as if she was by no means entirely convinced, but the girl had arrived now and it was a case of making the best of a bad job. She seemed to think Dr. McIntyre had been unduly optimistic, but commented drily:

'Oh, well, we'll see, my dear.' She turned in a businesslike way to Cameron. 'Well, we'd better be getting along now, Blair. You did give Deirdre lunch?'

He merely nodded, and moved to the boot of his own car to remove the girl's luggage.

He bestowed it aboard the jeep, together with the rest of Deirdre's impedimenta, and then when she had climbed up into the seat beside the driving seat stood looking in at her with a curious glint in his eyes.

'I'll be seeing you both,' he said, and walked away before Deirdre had a chance to thank him for the amount of time he had devoted to her and her well-being.

Hanging on tightly as the utility bowled away along the road, Deirdre knew she had never travelled in anything approaching a vehicle like this before. She looked round at Mrs. Liddle and felt impelled to put the question to her:

'Do you always travel at this kind of speed?'

Mrs. Liddle answered immediately.

'Have to. I'd never have enough time to spare to crawl along.' Her reply was terse, but nevertheless the truck slowed a little, and Deirdre drew a deep breath and felt as if her stomach slid back into position. 'You'd better unpack and just settle in this afternoon,' she suggested. 'You've had a long journey, and it's a different climate up here from the coast. You'll get accustomed to it, I've no doubt.'

'Yes,' Deirdre agreed. 'Yes, thank you, Mrs. Liddle. But,' she added determinedly, 'I would like to watch how you grade today, then perhaps I won't be too useless tomorrow.'

The relief in her companion's expression was very apparent. She took time off from studying the road ahead and the bouncing effect the truck had on it and glanced sideways approvingly at the new hand. 'You know, Deirdre,' she said, 'I don't need you to tell me I'm rushing things too much – myself as well as you. I know it without anyone telling me. But my contracts have to be finished on schedule, and farmers, you know, simply can't wait. Their tobacco must be ready when the sales begin, and Betty's illness has put me back nearly three weeks.'

'It was bad luck for you, certainly,' Deirdre murmured in reply. 'But it was also my good fortune that Dr. McIntyre is your doctor as well as mine.'

It had certainly seemed the answer to a somewhat difficult problem when Dr. McIntyre had made the suggestion that she could contact the woman by her side. He had admitted that he would prefer it if she could go away somewhere where she would have nothing to do but just laze in the sun, and be adequately looked after for six months or so. But as this was impossible the tobacco farm might do her a very great deal of good. The grading would not be too strenuous, and he seemed to have a fairly high opinion of Mrs. Liddle. She might be a bit rough and tough, but she had a good heart, and in any case beggars couldn't be choosers, and it was vitally necessary that Deirdre should have some sort of a change, and that she should get away from all reminders of her illness, and her long period of convalescence, for a little while. If it didn't work, well then, they would have to try and fix something else. But there was no real reason why it shouldn't work.

Deidre took his advice, as she had taken it once

before in her life when everything had gone badly wrong. For it was he who had broken the news to her when she came back from boarding school, dazed and brokenhearted, and too late even to see her parents for the last time, and with so little money that she had been glad to accept the job he found for her at the local library.

Now, at nineteen, she had to begin a new life for the second time ... a vastly different one, unless her first impressions were entirely wrong, from anything she had lived before. She had been content enough before, with the new friends she made and the tennis parties. Being good at tennis she received lots of invitations, and it was at one of them that she contracted her bad bout of pneumonia. A sudden shower, tropical and drenching, had sent them all, wet through, scurrying for shelter, and as the temperature lowered dramatically and there was no opportunity to change out of soaking garments the damage was done. It proved that she would have to be sensible about taking risks in future, but with someone like Mrs. Liddle to work for that might not be quite so easy.

'Do you know anything about tobacco, Deirdre?' Mrs. Liddle asked. 'Have you seen or handled it at all?'

Hanging on a little tighter to the edge of the bouncing seat, Deirdre glanced sideways at her interrogator.

'No,' she stated baldly, 'I haven't. But,' she

added hopefully, 'I'm sure I can learn.'

Mrs. Liddle decided there was no point in wasting valuable time and began instructing her straight away.

'You should understand, Deirdre, that there are a great many different grades of tobacco, and while actually working you stand at long benches rather like study tables. Every farm varies in the provision of actual working equipment, of course, but most of us use a slightly flat wooden bench with the top edge partitioned off into box-like sections, actually not at all unlike a cutlery drawer in the kitchen dresser.' Here Mrs. Liddle took one hand off the wheel and demonstrated by drawing patterns in the air. 'There are usually eight or nine of these sections, depending on the size of the farm, and the number of different species a farm is growing.'

She went on to describe the tobacco being taken in armfuls from the stacked bulk leaf, and laid on the benches, where it was examined, a leaf at a time, and classified. It would be Deirdre's job to assist this classification, and unless she was quick and apt she would not be much use. But, possibly because of the girl's anxious expression, she was kind enough to add that there was no reason to believe she wouldn't be very quick and apt indeed.

Deidre was relieved when she fell silent at last, and for the last part of the journey she was able to lean back against the hot seat and close her eyes against the glare of the sun, and she only opened them again when Mrs. Liddle uttered a sound which indicated that something unusual had occurred, and she let her eyelids flutter upwards wearily and saw that a group of buildings had come into view, and as the truck was slowing it was an indication that they had arrived.

The truck came to a standstill before a large, shed-like structure, set a small distance from a group of similar structures. Mrs. Liddle jumped out and lifted Deirdre's heavy suitcase over the tail-board as easily as if it had no weight at all, and Deirdre climbed out too, although much more stiffly and slowly than her companion. She looked around her as she stood on the ground, feeling as if the earth was wavering from sheer fatigue, and her heart sank because the place appeared deserted, there were no crops to be harvested and only a few trees, and of fellow human beings there appeared to be a curious dearth.

'Well, my dear, here we are,' Mrs. Liddle exclaimed. 'I expect you're saying thank goodness. I'm afraid I've talked an awful lot, and you really weren't in a mood to listen, were you?' There was kindness and humour in her tone, however, and for the first time Deirdre felt very, very slightly drawn towards her.

She followed the trousered figure into the house, and found herself in a somewhat curious living-room, with curtains at the far end concealing what she later discovered were four cell-like cubicles. The curtains, however, were vividly coloured, and were stirring gently in the breeze from the open windows. Everything looked very clean and immaculate, although somewhat austere, and there was the very minimum of furniture without the overall appearance striking too spartan a note.

Mrs. Liddle pointed to the end cubicle, and told her it was hers.

'That's where you sleep,' she said. 'The shower is outside, built on as an annexe. This is a bulkhead used for the storing of tobacco before it's graded.'

To Deirdre it all seemed very strange indeed. Mrs. Liddle managed to smile at her in a friendly way.

'I'll leave you to change,' she said, and pointed out one of the other buildings. 'You'll find us over there when you're ready.'

Deirdre nodded. 'I won't be long.'

Left alone, she unlocked a case, located a blouse and skirt and some flat-heeled shoes, and put them on, glad to be free of her travel-stained garments. Then she drew a long breath and stepped outside the cubicle, pausing for a moment in the strong sunshine before crossing to the unknown hut.

CHAPTER TWO

SPRAWLING at ease with her back to a post, Deirdre ate a huge lunch sandwich slowly, and let her gaze rest on the thin haze of heat that overhung the farm at midday. Her glance wandered and took in the line of trees that cut through the property, framing the small creek that wound a leisurely way through the paddocks and the arid pastures. It was in the creek that they all swam in the evenings, when work was over, and sought refreshment for mind and body. . . . All, that is, except Deirdre, for the water was cold, and her state of health did not yet permit her to take any risks, certainly not when they involved relaxation.

She wondered that she had ever thought it an unattractive landscape, for it was curiously attractive when one got to know it. Having finished her meal, she lay on her back luxuriating in the sun's warmth, and Mrs. Liddle came across to her and stood looking down at her.

'Are you coming into town with us tomorrow morning, Deirdre?' she asked. 'Everyone goes on Saturday.'

'No . . . No, I don't think so,' Deirdre answered slowly, not having thought about it before. Then she went on more decidedly: 'I'd rather not, if you don't mind. I want to shampoo my hair, and there are a hundred other things I want to do. Having been so busy learning to grade I've let everything else slip, and I simply must do something about my hair. It smells like a tobacco barn!'

'Everyone else smells that way, too. Throughout the season one lives, smells, and even eats tobacco, so don't worry if your hair has acquired the same taint.'

'Still, I think I'll stay at home.'

Marge, one of the girls, looked amazed by this decision. The other two, who were lounging on a bench, also looked rather surprised. It was quite obvious they were looking forward to their trip to town. They were attractive girls, Edna in particular, and although she dressed like Mrs. Liddle she managed somehow to convey the impression that she was managing to enjoy everything that came her way. Marge, young and brash, looked equally confident, but Norma was much more thoughtful and quiet. They were both Cairns girls, and had known Mrs. Liddle all their lives.

Henry, the youngest Brandt boy, who had brought their lunch across from the house, was sharing it with them, and he added his contribution to the conversation.

'You might even see Blair, Edna, and make a date with him for the movies ... if you're lucky!' His voice was teasing, but his eyes were admiring.

'I might,' she agreed.

Mrs. Liddle broke in.

'Don't think I'm being awkward, Edna, but I'll give you the same piece of advice I'd give Deirdre here if it was necessary. Blair Cameron has the reputation for making his own rules. You may think you're frightfully experienced, but she'll be a clever girl who catches Blair. The only thing in his favour is that he doesn't make the smallest pretence. Most girls know where they stand with him, and it's as well that you should do the same.'

Edna looked faintly bored, as if the information was of no real interest to her, but Deirdre, who had been waiting to hear something of her luncheon companion of the previous Monday, wanted to pursue the subject.

'I didn't like him,' she confessed. 'And what is there so extraordinary about him that you have to warn people about him? I suppose he's handsome, in a way that certainly doesn't appeal to me, and it's fairly obvious that he thinks quite a lot of himself. Bill Darrell is much nicer.'

She could feel them all staring hard at her.

'Do you honestly mean that you didn't find him attractive?' Mrs. Liddle demanded, voicing the amazement of the rest of them. 'Quite *extraordinarily* attractive, I mean? *Different*, if you follow me.'

Deirdre shook her head.

'Then you're the first girl of your age I've encountered who's taken up such an attitude,' Mrs. Liddle told her. 'I personally can't explain the attraction he has – for men as well as women! – but it's there. You could call it glamour, I suppose, or else it's something to do with that strange hardness of his.'

'But if he's only a farmer,' Deirdre protested, 'he can't be as glamorous as all that. Wealth is generally a necessary perquisite for such a label,' she added.

The older woman glanced at Henry with a grin. 'You hear that, Henry?' she asked. 'Tell Deirdre what you're worth!' But Henry only smiled his wide smile at them, and remained silent.

Deirdre glanced a little curiously at the spreading farm buildings behind them. She knew that this was a big farm, and that it had a great deal of machinery and many outbuildings. But still, to her it didn't exactly cry wealth. It wasn't modern enough.

Mrs. Liddle followed her glance and sought to put her right.

'Don't get yourself confused, Deirdre. That's the house that was built when they first came here to open up the country. They were hard times, then, very hard. . . . But time doesn't stand still, and you could say they're no longer hard.'

But she sounded a little wistful, Deirdre thought, nevertheless. She snapped out of her wistfulness the next second, however, by ordering them back to work, and as they all scurried ahead of her Deirdre and she fell behind. Deirdre heard her say something rather curious to herself, as if she was reflecting on the conversation that had just taken place.

'I wonder. ... I wonder?' she said. 'I wonder whether Lexia Olsen will get him in the end?'

'Get who?' Deirdre asked.

But Mrs. Liddle merely stared at her and said nothing.

Proceeding towards her work bench, Deirdre paused for a moment, gazing about her. It all seemed so welcoming, so familiar, now. She remembered how panic-stricken she had been when she first arrived, but now the panic had given place to interest. Unknown words, mahogany, brights, lugs, sponge, had flown about her. The most dreaded word in tobacco farming had also made its appearance, blue mould. But with all the technical jargon issuing from her lips the very timbre of Mrs. Liddle's voice had altered and taken on an almost caressing note every time she spoke about tobacco, and then grown crisp again as she had shown Deirdre how to go about grading it.

Deirdre had taken a deep drawn breath, and wondered again, a little panicky, if she would ever learn the intricate, seemingly involved process, and be able to, among all the maze of technicality, decide which grade belonged to which. Then she had sharply stopped herself thinking along those lines.

Of course she would find she could manage: she knew she would have to.

Preparing to roll out of bed at the usual six o'clock next morning, then realizing that it was Saturday, Deirdre snuggled back into the bedclothes; the faint noise of people up and about adding a delicious feeling of luxury to the action. As she was drifting off to sleep again, a head came round the curtain. 'Are you coming over to breakfast, Deirdre?' she was asked.

She half raised herself, pulling the net aside to enable her to see Edna. 'Will it be in order if I miss it? I think I'll be lazy this morning,' She looked inquiringly at her visitor, not as yet conversant with what was permissible, and what was not, as this was her first Saturday morning.

Her look held admiration as well as inquiry, as she came more wide awake and looked fully at the girl standing in the curtained opening, the sunshine from the side window splashing about her. It may have been early in the morning, but Edna carried still the aura of glossy magazines; of expert grooming; of casual perfection, and she smiled at the glance of approval being accorded her, departing with a casual wave of her hand.

'Do whatever suits you, my dear. That's what living is for,' Edna replied easily, and dropping the curtain behind her she drifted away.

'I wish I could be like her,' Deirdre thought enviously, but accepted at the same time that you were what you were, and behaved as upbringing and environment made you behave. Did what you knew you had to do and hoped for the best. She was interrupted again as she was slipping back into sleep by the brisk voice of Mrs. Liddle.

'You'd better have this, Deirdre. You can go back to sleep afterwards.' A cup of tea was handed through the mosquito net. 'I don't want you going sick on me again, you know.'

Deirdre smiled as she took the tea and generous helping of toast. 'You don't frighten me a bit now,' she said, pushing the net further out of her way. 'I've known you for a whole week, remember, and that makes a difference. You look much more cheerful, too, than you did the day we first met. Are we making up time at all, and have I learnt to grade to suit you?'

The answer, when it came, accompanied by the rattle of curtain rings sliding shut, was reflective, considering. 'Yes ... yes ...s, we're doing very well, and you're coming along fine. Also, Deirdre, your yourself look a different girl from the one who came up here. You haven't accumulated much weight as yet, but you've lost that fragile look. Yes, I said fragile,' she repeated as Deirdre protested. 'You have colour in your cheeks now, and even a little suntan. We'll make a changed girl of you in a couple of months, given half a chance.'

She went off indifferent to any answer forthcoming, leaving Deirdre to drink her tea.

Feeling disinclined for further sleep, Deirdre lay gazing out of her window. She could see clear down to the creek with only a corner of the bulkshed to obscure her view. The sky was its usual blue, luminous, thought Deirdre, trying to think of a descriptive colour to suit it; so different from the brazen tropical blue of home. And the quiet; the stillness, silence, of this age-old bushland was something actually felt. Used all her life as a city dweller to noise of all variety about her, this stillness was strange. Even when she had been away at school, noise was a thing taken for granted, as the college had been situated in the heart of the town. She suddenly realized that she was thinking of school life – for the first time since her parents had been killed – without the old emptiness and longing.

She had washed her hair, dried and set it; did the hundred odd – or so it seemed to her – things she had told the others she had let slide for the past week, and was lying full length on a cane lounger which she had dragged outside under a big shady tree. A book in her lap was unheeded when the old truck, making its usual loud commotion, pulled in just on lunch time. Edna and Norma flopped down on the grass in the shade beside her, while Marge fetched Mrs. Liddle a deck-chair into which she thankfully subsided, stretching her feet and easing off her shoes.

'Did you get your date, Edna?' Deirdre felt impelled to ask.

'I don't know if you're referring to any special date, Deirdre. However, I did get one. I'm going to the pictures with Stan Bolton. Also, I'm giving fair warning, I'm going to sleep all afternoon and will take very unkindly to being disturbed.'

'So am I,' Mrs. Liddle put in. 'But you have an invitation, Deirdre – you, Marge, and Norma. Henry is taking you in to tennis. Blair said he would see you all safely home, and as it was he who invited you, he'll look after you.'

'You know, Mrs. Liddle,' Norma broke in, 'I can't understand Blair asking us. He smiles at me when we meet, and I've graded at his place all the time I've been with you, but I didn't expect he would even remember my name. He's never actually spoken directly to me.'

'Nonsense, Norma. You've been at his farm for three years now, of course he knows your name. I can tell you,' acid was in the tone, 'there's nothing he doesn't know when it concerns him, even if in only a small way. I expect he realizes that there's not a great deal of entertainment in such a small place as this, and knowing Deirdre plays tennis, he thought to ask her. Depend on it, that's the reason. Blair can be very kind when he takes the trouble; if only he does take the trouble,' she ended up dryly.

Deirdre had been listening attentively. 'Do we go out to Mr. Cameron's farm to grade ... ' she faltered, and coloured faintly as all eyes turned her way.

'Of course we do. Haven't I told you?' The older woman's voice was crisp. 'We've done his grading for as long as I've graded, and really, Deirdre, I couldn't think about who you were talking about. Mr. Cameron, indeed! ... It's a funny thing,' she went on. 'I say we're going out to Brandt's or Wilson's and other farms by their surnames, but I always – and I think this applies to everyone – say that I'm going out to Blair's. I hadn't given it a thought before. Well, lunch is ready.' She got up from her chair as a cooee floated across from the house.

Waiting in the shade of the same big tree in front of their quarters for Henry to collect them and take them into town, Deirdre looked down at the other two lounging on the grass in their white tennis clothes – shorts and shirts in their case, a pleated dress in hers – and thought gratefully how lucky she had been to fall among these people. It could so easily have been different – alone, having to come to a strange town, knowing no one, even though Dr. Mac had known and had sent her here.

'Can you play tennis, Deirdre?' Marge's voice broke through her thoughts. 'I like it, but I'm not terribly good. Norma is, though, and so is Mrs. Liddle, only she doesn't play a great deal now.'

'Yes, I expect I play reasonably well, Marge, but then I had special coaching at school. I'm not really good; just steady.'

'Here's Henry,' Norma ejaculated, as she rose slowly from the ground. Deirdre smiled widely, and Norma, knowing what she was thinking, grinned back.

It was a standing joke among them, this habit of Norma's of sitting down when it was at all possible. Even when grading, at which most of them stood, she could always manage to scrounge a high stool or contrive to find something on which to sit.

All in, and the doors slammed – Deirdre wondered if everyone up here slammed car doors; she couldn't remember noticing it back home – the big vehicle sped along the farm track to enter a road which was at times closed in by bush, but more often lined by big tobacco farms on both sides. Not having seen the little township since her arrival, Deirdre looked round her with new eyes when they entered it. It was still only a tiny place, but there seemed to be as much here to amuse and entertain, as at home, except perhaps on a smaller scale.

She was a little shy at the warmth of the greetings showered upon her as Henry pulled the car to a stop beside the courts, and knew that she would not remember names, but would have to sort them out as she went along. Racquet in hand, her cardigan pulled close, she edged her way down to the far end of the pavilion where the sunlight made a blaze of gold against the deep shade of the shelter, wishing now that she had brought something a little warmer than the thin sweater she had flung round her shoulders.

'Nobody thinks to introduce me! Just the slave around to boil the billy, that's me!' The tone and attitude of the youth who had fallen into the seat beside her belied his words. Young, thick-set, very fair, he was so much a replica of the set she was used to in Cairns that she was instantly at her ease with him.

'I'm Charles Wilson,' he went on. 'You'll see more of me, as you do our tobacco too, you know.'

'Oh, that will be nice, going to a farm where I actually know someone. But tell me, what did you mean by saying you were boiling the billy?' Deirdre inquired.

'Well ... ll, I was making a dashed great fire under a kerosene tin full of water. We need plenty of liquid when afternoon tea time comes along.'

'No, truly, are we really going to have tea made out in the open in a big tin? I thought that had gone out a hundred years ago.'

Charles took in the amazed delight on the face beside him. 'Yes, we truly are,' he mimicked her. 'Do you think you'll be able to drink smoked billy tea?' His tone changed abruptly. 'But, my deah, how primitive! One can't drink tea with that awful taste. Haven't you any civilization at all up here?'

He looked surprised as Deirdre collapsed into giggles. 'Have I said something funny?' he wanted to know in a stern voice, while his eyes sparkled. 'I assure you that's exactly how one of our southern visitors phrased it.' He grinned then, suddenly, matching the smile in his eyes, white teeth flashing against brown skin, and said engagingly: 'There, I would much rather have your reaction to billy tea than the other . . .' he broke off as a car pulled up, doors slammed, and a babble of voices rose above the soft hum of conversation. 'Here they are,' he said. 'We'll be starting soon.'

Deirdre instinctively straightened as one voice, though low, came through to her above all others.

Another car travelling fast, very fast, with much too much speed to pull up with decorum, slid to a stop, braking hard, at their side of the shelter; and out of its royal blue low-slung elegance stepped a girl in white tennis clothes.

'Oh, and here's Lexia, too. Right on cue.' Charles's voice had an edge to it.

'She's lovely!' Deirdre exclaimed, and she honestly thought so. If Mrs. Liddle had been thinking of her in connection with Blair Cameron last night then she had every reason for wishing to speculate. They would make a perfect pair, tall and lithe, like a couple of Greek gods.

'Look, there's Norma and Tony starting to play against one another!' Charles sounded much more diverted. This time there was warmth and appreciation in his smile.

'Who's that playing with them, Charles?' Deirdre asked, her eyes on the court in question.

'Mr. and Mrs. Carr. They're good, aren't they? They play in the tournaments. Except for Blair and, I suppose, Lexia, they're the best players we have. If only we had a couple more . . . just to beat Nerada once would make me happy.'

She turned, really surprised at his fervent tone. 'You sound as if you meant that, Charles,' she remarked. 'Does tennis mean a lot to you?'

'Yes, as a matter of fact it does. We have a court out at the farm, and I can generally manage to get together a representative team. But I think it would be nice to be victorious occasionally.' He grinned engagingly sideways at her. 'Don't look so solemn. I really don't mind not winning, and one can always hope.'

Her attention returned to the courts. She glanced from Norma to Tony and asked Charles softly: 'Do they know each other well?' catching a passing look between the pair as they crossed over.

Her companion's eyes followed her gaze. 'Yes, the rapport between them shows sometimes, doesn't it? However,' he shrugged, 'different nationality, different traditions; so whether anything will come of it is anybody's guess.' With a murmured excuse, he rose as his name was called and went away to retrieve his racquet.

When she walked on to the court in her turn, she was as nervous as any beginner, but actually playing tennis, she hadn't a thought for anything else. Returning to the pavilion with her partner after winning six love and thinking nothing of it as their opponents had been only young players, she was surprised to be caught up in a bear-hug by Charles.

'Why, Deirdre,' he stammered excitedly, 'you're good! Why didn't you say so?' He turned to the cluster of players facing him, an arm still clasped round her shoulders. 'What price Nerada this year, eh, you fellers?' he beamed.

Astonishment kept her motionless, indeed not understanding Charles's exuberance, then she saw Blair's eyes. They began at the top of her head and continued downwards, stopping for a studied second at her shoulders on which her companion's arm still remained. Suddenly everyone was talking.

'No, really, I'm not that good,' she protested. 'I just have a steady game.' She gently disengaged herself from the arm around her and went to sit beside Norma. Picking up her discarded cardigan, she pulled it tightly about her; for some unknown reason she was trembling.

Abruptly the light jumper was lifted from her, and even as she swung round she knew who would be standing there. Blair held out a huge white sweater.

'Put your arms in.'

As she made no move to obey, those glinting eyes came up to her face, and taking in the challenge of them, Deirdre could only put first one arm and then the other into sleeves which were held for her. For a

39

fleeting instant a hand touched her throat as the top button was fastened, then she knew he was behind her no longer. The whole episode had taken a mere half-minute, but Deirdre sat there, her head down, feeling that she must be the cynosure of all eyes.

A sidelong glance at Norma told her that her attention was centred entirely on the courts, another quick look round made her realize that there were no glances her way. She drew in a deep breath and saw that afternoon tea was already in the process of being prepared and was taking up the time of most of the women not actually engaged in playing tennis.

Reassured, her gaze swung back, to hesitate as she saw that one person was looking at her. Her eyes met eyes of light hazel which slowly looked her over, then turned away without a gleam of recognition; the only one there who had not smiled at her, Deirdre realized, and shifted to sit closer to Norma as her glance fell away from the white-clad back. She drew the big cardigan tight, hugging its warmth to her, smelling the faint tang of cigarettes, and another elusive perfume to which she could put no name.

Later that night, before going to bed, she leant against the wall near her small window and watched as the silhouettes of the trees along the creek bed lost their vivid outline against the paleness of the night sky. Abruptly the gleam of stars made their appearance. She gave a sigh of sheer contentment, turned, and, early as it was, climbed into bed, pulling the covers high to her chin. Her gaze went to the big cardigan lying folded on a chair beside the dressing table. She had not spoken to Blair again that afternoon, but half taking off the warm garment as they were making their departure, had met his eyes across the intervening space. Somehow she had found herself, sweater and all, safely in the corner of the car, as Henry pulled away with his usual spurt of gravel.

Now, in bed, drowsily listening to the shrill call of crickets as they went about their nocturnal pursuits, she resolutely shifted her thoughts from Mrs. Liddle's warning. Mrs. Liddle, who invariably minded her own business, but who had stated so unequivocally her knowledge of Blair. But all her resolutions couldn't prevent the image of his face drifting before her as she went over the borderland of sleep.

CHAPTER THREE

FALLING low behind the distant hills, with only thin shafts of its golden light spilling across the water, a reminder that night swallowed quickly the short evenings up here in the far north, Deirdre wrapped herself more warmly in her towelling beach robe and watched the sun hang right on the edge of the world. The Brandt boys were swimming in the centre of the creek, with Marge as proficient as they were. Norma, as usual, was just sitting, making no effort at all as she allowed the water to wash over her. Deirdre had had her brief dip, careful to run no risk of catching a chill, and was lazing; knowing now that the bushlands had a fascination all of their own.

She dragged her eyes from the horizon, empty now of the globe of gold, with only a stain of crimson to mark its passing, and looked at Norma as she came from the water. 'Coming up to our quarters, Deirdre?' she asked, stooping to pick up her towel. 'I've had enough.'

The younger girl nodded, and rising fell into step. 'Norma. . . .' Norma looked round as Deirdre hesitated. Deirdre began again.

'About tomorrow night. I've never been to a dance . . . I mean, one like this. What does one do, sit round and wait to be asked to dance?'

Norma laughed and her voice came partly obscured by the rough towelling her head was taking. 'I don't imagine you need bother about it, Deirdre. Just go and enjoy yourself. You certainly won't lack for partners.' She shook her hair back and her words came more distinctly. 'Are you playing tennis in the afternoon? I know Charles has been keeping the Brandt telephone ringing all week for you.'

Deidre shook her head. 'No, I'm going to rest. I expect I'm more careful than is needed, but do you know, Norma, I still have nightmares about getting ill again, so I'm going to be sure rather than sorry from now on.'

Dressed, they strolled across to the house and took their places at the big table. Deirdre went on with her meal, hearing the talk about her but with thoughts entirely occupied with the following night. Somehow she couldn't quite see Blair at a small Saturday night dance, and of course she couldn't ask, so had no way of knowing if he would be present or not.

Walking back to the quarters later through dense ebony shadows, Deirdre was amazed at how dark it could really be up here on a moonless night. She couldn't remember experiencing darkness quite like this before, and guessed that in towns and cities lights being switched on at first blush of evening was responsible for this lack of knowledge. Pushing these wandering thoughts aside, she made herself ask

43

what she had been wanting to find out for the past week, and out the words tumbled with a rush. 'Norma, what shall I do with that white cardigan?'

Norma didn't ask, 'What white cardigan?' She returned casually, 'I'd pack it up and take it in tomorrow night and drop it into Blair's car. You can leave your thank-yous until the next time you see him to talk to. Will that do?'

'Yes, it'll do, perfectly, thanks. Do you know, Norma, I'm very glad I came up here and met you!'

Moving this way and that, trying to see the whole of her dress in the tiny mirror as she smoothed it around her hips Deirdre knew that it suited her. The faintly darker pattern of leaves on the blue shining satin cotton caused it to shimmer as she moved and the full skirt falling to an inch above her knees was just right for dancing, not as short as it might have been, but still, how she liked it. Her brown hair, ordinary, what the cosmetic blurbs called mousy, nevertheless added a beauty to her expectant party look as it hung, shining, swinging free about her face. Another last glance in the mirror and she gathered up her evening bag and walked to the living-room where the others were gathered.

Mrs. Liddle smiled at her, but after a closer look, remarked crisply, 'You'd better go get something warm for coming home, Deirdre.'

'It's not cold tonight,' Deirdre protested.

'It will be at twelve o'clock or thereabouts,' was what she was told in the same curt voice.

Deirdre shrugged and walked obediently back to her cubicle, took down a small velvet jacket, folding it over her arm.

Henry arrived in his father's big car, but as Henry was driving it, the arrival was attended by the usual screech of brakes and scattering of gravel. They all crowded in, careful of their dresses. Deirdre sat back in her corner watching the countryside fly by, illuminated by the thin sickle of a new moon, and thinking how different were her feelings now from the day when she had arrived. A tiny smile curved her lips as she reflected on the months that lay before her, once anticipated as something to be got through, while now. . . .

'All out!' Henry called cheerfully, as he expertly parked the car alongside a number of others stationary on the grass.

Stepping out and standing beside her door, Deirdre waited as Norma cast a searching look over the assembled vehicles. 'I can't see Blair, he can't be here yet,' she said quietly.

'Will he be coming?' Deirdre inquired.

Norma's voice held real amusement. 'Of course he will, unless he's ill . . . and I've never heard of Blair being sick yet. It's Saturday night!'

As if being Saturday night explained everything, Deirdre thought in exasperation.

They followed slowly along behind the rest of the party towards the dance hall. On entering, it didn't appear large to Deirdre, but as she walked across the floor she realized that she had better watch out while dancing. It was as slippery as glass. Accosted from all sides with greetings, gaily called both softly and with gusto, answered in like manner by Marge, Deirdre, and Edna, she was glad to slip thankfully on to the bench against the wall beside Norma, smiling a little shyly at faces she did know.

When the orchestra started she watched Charles cross the floor towards her, and as she went into his arms, decided it was good to be dancing again after so long. The music was swinging, the floor excellent, and all her partners seemed outstandingly good. She concentrated on just enjoying herself.

It wasn't until nearly eleven o'clock that, glancing over her current partner's shoulder, she looked suddenly into glinting blue eyes, saw them follow her as she drifted past. Circling the floor, her gaze swept back over the dancers' heads, searching for that tall dark one; and saw two ... the raven darkness of a man's head bent over the creamy blonde fairness of his partner. Hearts don't suddenly plunge sickeningly, she admonished herself. It's physically impossible; nevertheless, the bright lights, the pulsing music of a moment ago were no longer the joyous things they had been. Her smile came automatically with her thanks as her partner escorted her back to her seat, then froze. Bending over Mrs. Liddle, casually clearing the vacant seat beside her of its accumulated evening accessories, the subject of her thoughts was gracefully subsiding into its now empty space.

She sat in her seat, silent, tense, taking no part whatever in the conversation; conscious only of that figure beyond – oh, so sure of himself, completely at his ease, she thought wrathfully, knowing what her own feelings were – as he laughed and parried questions hurled at him on his lateness.

The music began, she saw him rise, step across Mrs. Liddle and hold out his hand. In his arms on the floor they danced slowly; the rigid band at her waist drawing her even closer as the music went soft. He didn't speak, and Deirdre couldn't. All too soon it was over. She looked upwards, stars in her eyes, but Blair barely glanced her way as he seated her with a casual nod, dropping down again beside Mrs. Liddle. That worthy was listening grimly to a hotly protesting Marge who swung round as the others settled down. 'We have to leave now,' she told them. 'Mrs. Liddle is going over to the Paynes' for a cup of tea and she says we have to come with her.'

'Couldn't Henry escort us across when the dance finishes, please, Mrs. Liddle?' Norma begged.

'Well, I suppose he can, if you can find him.' The older woman spoke slowly, unwillingly.

He wasn't in sight and Norma was wondering if she could send someone to find him when Blair's soft voice cut in, 'I'll look after the girls, and bring them over to you when it finishes here, Mrs. Liddle.'

There was a concerted movement as all eyes turned his way, astonishment apparent on every face. They knew Mrs. Liddle's opinion of him. It was one of the first things they were warned about when starting work with her up here. As she said, any young girl looking at him could be excused for having her dreams of conquest. But it wouldn't be her conquest, they were told, very dryly, and their mentor wanted no complications, so got in first. Not than any young girl in her employ – or for that matter, in any other employment – had ever been able to boast of a date with him.

Now he returned Mrs. Liddle's stare, his face bland and unconcerned, showing no interest whatever in the looks he was receiving from other directions.

'Very well, Blair. Just bring them across to Paynes' yourself.' Her voice was crisp, normal.

'I'll be both duenna and escort, and guarantee to deliver them safe and sound. Satisfied?' An eyebrow climbed as his eyes laughed at her.

'Of course, if you say so, Blair,' she answered smoothly, and they sat astonished, silent, and watched her walk away.

'Well!' Norma ejaculated. She turned to find Blair watching her.

'Mrs. Liddle and I know each other from way back,' he remarked cryptically, and taking out his cigarettes paid no more attention to them.

For Deirdre the next hour fled. Their watchdog danced with none of them. He saw them on to the floor, crossed the hall to Lexia's party, returning to sit with them during the intervals, silent, smoking continually. At the last dance he stayed in his seat, rose as the Anthem swelled out, pulled on his jacket at its conclusion, and waited patiently for them to collect bags and other belongings, then herded all three of them towards the door.

'For all the world like a mother duck!' Norma's shocked whisper echoed in Deirdre's ear.

Henry attached himself to the party as they sauntered past the parked cars. 'Oh!' Deirdre's hand flew to her mouth. 'Oh, your cardigan, I forgot it.' She looked at Blair. 'I have it in Henry's car,' she told him, and made to run back.

A hand shot out, detaining her. Blair turned to the younger man. 'Walk the girls slowly to the Paynes', Henry,' he said in that low voice of his. 'We'll catch you up,' then he turned, his hand still clasping her arm.

Not waiting for him to open the car door upon reaching it, Deirdre hurriedly jerked at the release and groped inside for the big parcel. Picking up her coat as well, she turned to hand him the package. He was standing in the triangular opening formed by the partly opened door, the faintly lit, now moonless night making him appear fantastically big. Taking hold of the cardigan, he dropped it back on to the seat, then possessing himself of the coat from a suddenly nerveless hand, he put her arms into it and slowly turned her to face him.

The arm that had held her so firmly on the dance floor earlier was just as firm now about her waist, and she felt her chin tipped gently upwards. Slowly again, his mouth came lower and rested carefully, full upon her own. She stood in the circle of his arms, allowing his kiss, knowing also that she should be angry and tell him so; but the feeling of warmth and happiness, and utter security, held her. Then abruptly there was no thought at all of security as gentleness departed, the hold around her tightened, and she was left with only the ecstasy of his kiss filling her completely.

It was the man who withdrew first, setting her gently back against the car. The big button of her velvet coat was fastened, the brown fingers touching her throat as they had on a previous occasion, then she found herself standing clear. The car door slammed and she was walking beside him, walking, if unsteadily, across the dew-spangled grass, one of his hands at her elbow, the other carrying a large brown paper parcel.

They caught up the others, Deirdre moving in a daze, unable to speak herself or take in coherently the conversation about her. To their surprise Mrs. Liddle was outside waiting for them.

'I didn't expect you to be ready so early. We could have hurried more,' Norma told her contritely.

But the older woman was not impatient at being kept waiting, as she normally would have been. In fact she seemed quite happy. 'It didn't really matter,' she answered them placidly. 'I've been making arrangements. We've decided on an excursion tomorrow. Jack and Enid,' she gestured to the Paynes, 'have to go out to the Walsh to see a farmer, so we've decided to make a day of it and have a picnic.'

'Is this a private picnic or can anyone join in?' Henry interjected.

'I daresay you can come, Henry. Your car will be very useful.'

His laconic, 'Well, thanks very much, ma'am, for such an enthusiastic invitation. I'd be charmed,' brought a smile to even Mrs. Liddle's normally dour face, as she probably realized how her invitation had sounded, but it brought forth no apology. As far as she was concerned, everybody up here knew her; they took her as they found her or not at all.

'If this is an invite-yourself affair, I may as well add my name,' Blair's voice joined in. 'Maybe my car will come in useful, too.'

'Oh, Blair! Would you really like to come? Good! I needn't bring my old jalopy then, and we'll be able to travel in comfort.' Satisfied as to her own plans, and not one to bother about others, she began to stride off, calling back over her shoulder, 'We've made arrangements about food, Blair. Just bring yourself, and of course, your car!'

Deirdre sat in her corner as the car raced through the night. It slowed a little, perforce, at a trenchant sentence directed to its driver by the tense figure of Mrs. Liddle by his side, but Deirdre had no thoughts of speed or the lack of it tonight, and determinedly pushed them aside for the moment, too, the memory of what had occurred in this very conveyance's shadow just a few short minutes ago.

Alone at last, she changed into pyjamas and climbed into bed, trying to bring some kind of order to the chaos of her whirling thoughts. In her experience – which she was the first to admit was a limited one – men who kissed you at least liked you. Blair's conduct so far to her made that assumption untenable.

She buried her burning face in the pillow, and was thankful for one thing at least. Her new-found friends knew nothing of the incident. She there and then resolved that they never would know, and that there would never be another such episode for them to hear of.

The rattle of curtain rings drawn briskly along their rods penetrated the exhausted sleep into which Deirdre had finally fallen. She sat up, startled, then relaxed as Mrs. Liddle's voice came, crisp, incisive. 'Breakfast is here, girls, come along and hurry up now. There's the food to be packed, and you can all help.'

Deirdre reached for her dressing-gown and

walked sleepily out to the big room to collect her tea and toast from one of the breakfast trays. Breakfast was brought across to their quarters on Sunday mornings; that way, Mrs. Liddle had explained to Deirdre when she had first arrived, it catered for all tastes. If you wanted to sleep, you slept. If you were hungry, food was available.

Sipping the very hot tea, she saw that Edna too was up and went to join her by the window.

'Are you going as well, Edna?' she asked.

'Mrs. Liddle says I am,' Edna yawned, 'so I expect I must be.'

Deirdre smiled at her. 'Don't pretend you're not happy with the prospect. Isn't it perfect picnic weather?' It was, and they leisurely consumed their simple breakfast, letting the early morning sunshine splash about them. After a minute or so, Deirdre asked her silent companion, 'Did you enjoy yourself last night, Edna? You were surrounded every time I caught a glimpse of you.'

Edna returned the younger girl's look with her Mona Lisa smile. 'And so were you, my dear. In fact, you were dancing in very exalted circles at one stage of the affair. Tell me, did you enjoy yourself?'

Willing her face to remain just ordinarily enthusiastic, with no sign of her real thoughts in evidence, Deirdre answered brightly, 'Yes, indeed I did! I've never enjoyed myself more. I dare say I didn't know more than perhaps half of my partners, but every one of them could certainly dance.'

'Yes, I've noticed that,' Edna answered. 'In all the small country towns I've travelled through it's the same. I expect they put more concentration into dancing, possibly because they haven't many other interests. Do you know, Deirdre,' she continued lazily, 'I've been seriously thinking that I might decide to stay here permanently. Would you think it likely that I might find a husband to keep me here?'

'Oh, Edna, you're incorrigible! A husband to keep you here indeed! What a way to talk of marriage! You don't have to try to find a husband; you meet someone one day . . . and well, there it is.' Yes, there it was indeed! Much good it would do her! Her voice was low as she went on, 'I'll bet that you, with your looks and charm, have had more than your share of men feel that way about you.'

Edna gave a low gurgle of laughter. 'Oh, Deirdre, you baby, but you do me good.' She yawned again and stretched, reaching for her towel and sponge-bag. 'I'm for the bathroom, but first, I expect, I'd better phone Stan as Mrs. Liddle has ordered me to do. Do you know, Deirdre,' she smiled across to where the older woman was grumbling at everyone as she hurried about the long room, packing cartons, 'this started out as a picnic between her and some friends, and now half of Limberg is going – all our Brandt boys and their parents, *and* their girls, *and* three cars from here; also, she informs me, Blair is putting in an appearance. I only hope she hasn't included Lexia. However, knowing her I don't expect she would do that.'

'Why wouldn't she, Edna? Doesn't Mrs. Liddle like Lexia?'

'I don't know if she cares for her one way or another, Deirdre. But she does dote on Blair and wouldn't care to see Lexia get him.'

'Dotes on Blair! Mrs. Liddle?' Deirdre couldn't keep the astonishment from her voice. 'Why, you yourself heard what she said, and for that matter, still says about him.'

Edna cut in, 'I know all that. However, what he does doesn't matter one hoot to her. It doesn't concern her. She still thinks the world of him. She always has . . .' she broke off, catching the look flung in her direction from the object of their discussion, made a little moue at Deirdre and strolled out on her way to the bathroom.

Deirdre sat on, dreaming, her gaze on the vast blue archway beyond the window. She turned with a start as Mrs. Liddle paused beside her, saying curtly, 'If you have nothing better to do than sit mooning, Deirdre, you might go over and help Mrs. Brandt.'

'Yes, of course, Mrs. Liddle. I'll dress and go right away,' she answered contritely.

Eventually everything was ready, order out of chaos, calm out of frenzied rushing, cars waiting. The three young girls stood beside their conveyance and crowded in as Bill, the older Brandt brother, slid into the driver's seat. About to let in the clutch, he clasped a hand suddenly to his forehead. 'Oh, my gosh,' he exclaimed, 'I forgot Yvonne's sun-cream!' He was out of the car in a flash, running back to the house.

'It's all right for you to laugh,' he told them, panting, when he returned, with a glance at the broadly grinning girls, and sent the car spinning after the others with the spurt of gravel Deirdre was now accustomed to when travelling with Henry – a family characteristic, evidently, she thought wryly – and handed over the tube of cream to be stowed in the glove compartment. 'But I'd be either coming back for it, or we'd be staying home. You know how Yvonne burns; and it was the last thing she said to me on the phone ... well,' his smile gleamed suddenly, 'practically the last,' he amended.

Eyeing the crowd already congregated as they all tumbled out of the cars, Edna caught Mrs. Liddle's glance and shrugged ruefully. 'Truly,' she said, 'there's no one like you for doing things on a grand scale once you get started. I'd hate to have you organizing me for the rest of my life!'

'I'd make a far better job of it than you seem to be doing,' was all the answer she received as the other walked away to begin organizing her own picnic.

Edna laughed. 'Well, I certainly asked for that,' she admitted.

Deirdre had seen the big car standing before the

house the moment they had arrived, and now saw Blair as he came from beyond it to deposit a large box into its capacious boot.

'Blair,' Mrs. Liddle called to him, 'I forgot to tell you about cream. I don't expect you thought to bring any?'

'Didn't you, though?' there was a touch of sarcasm in the smiling voice. 'For once you suppose wrong. I've even brought a bucket of fruit salad made with my own fair hands,' holding aloft a huge white container. 'Do you think it might come in handy too, like the cars?'

Norma answered Deirdre's glance of inquiry at the shout of laughter which went up. 'Blair's fruit salads are famous. He grows most tropical fruits on the farm, as does nearly everyone else. Only he adds something extra. Mrs. Liddle says cherry brandy, other people say different things; whatever they try, it's simply not the same as his. Blair only laughs and says, "Guess".'

Deirdre asked impulsively, 'What is he like, Norma? I mean, really like? What do you think of him?'

Gazing across at him to where he stood amid a laughing group. Norma hesitated, trying to find words. 'I don't know what to say to you, Deirdre,' she answered slowly. 'I really don't know him very well. I've graded at his farms for years, but we girls have nothing at all to do with him. We never go over to his house as we do at every other place. Mrs.

Liddle does, of course, but then she's known him all his life, his parents too. I suppose the majority of us girls grading for Mrs. Liddle went through a period at one time or another of having a crush on him. However, one can't keep on having a crush on someone who only treats one as a necessary part of the farm's furnishings.' She gave Deirdre a direct look before turning to the cars which were rapidly filling up, continuing a little breathlessly, 'I know he's fascinating, Deirdre, and, as Mrs. Liddle says, he does have a glamour surrounding him; but if I were you I would find my interests in Charles or Henry or any one of a dozen young men like them.' From Norma, the placid, even her tone carried an undercurrent of warning.

All too late, any warning now, much too late, Deirdre realized, knowing that whatever the outcome of this time up here, she would have to manage her life alone somehow. Not for her an interest in any of a dozen young men as Norma advised; they could mean nothing to her now. Last night had changed all that. She shrugged fatalistically. She would manage; she had before. . . .

Marge came up to them demanding to be told where Mrs. Liddle was. Leaving Norma to cope with what was to Marge an unsurmountable problem, Deirdre wandered across to the car in which they had travelled to town. Suddenly her breath stilled, she leant against the warm metal for support. Blair was beside her, close. He looked down, for once unsmiling. 'How are you going, Deirdre?' he asked gravely. 'Is it in one of the Brandts' cars?'

'Yes, thank you – Henry's.' She said no more, her face closed, her expression remote, as she looked past him into the distance.

His manner changed then; he walked still closer, his voice audible only to her. 'Apparently you have a partiality for Henry's car. Don't tell me it brings back pleasant memories ... maybe of last night?' There was an edge to his words.

Not understanding his meaning for one long moment, she gazed up at him, puzzled; then a burning tide of colour flamed from neck to forehead, and she hated him; hated him with all her heart for speaking so mockingly of something which to her had been so momentous. She turned, fumbling blindly for the door at her back – that same door she had also attempted to open last night. Brown fingers closed upon the groping hand, efficiently doing what was needed, and she was manipulated smoothly into the rear seat. Blair slid the door shut and stood with his back to it, detaining Bill as he made for the driving side. A swift all-encompassing glance at the small curled-up figure in her corner, and he waved Bill on, standing aside to allow the rest of the passengers to crowd in. Deirdre saw him give his casual half-salute and walk across to his own car, then they were moving and he was gone. She turned her face to the window.

'Isn't it fun to be going like this, right out of the

blue?' Yvonne's voice held contentment. 'I declare,' she went on, 'I'm going to have a wonderful time today.'

'That's because you didn't have to do any of the work in preparing for it, lazybones,' Bill broke in. 'You and Norma make a very good pair.'

Yvonne only smiled and settled back comfortably in her seat.

'How far is it to where we're going?' Deirdre asked of the man sitting beside her, knowing that she must make an effort to be sociable.

'About five miles, and I think it's just the place for a picnic. Good swimming, plenty of shade, idyllic surroundings. . . .' His voice went on and Deirdre leant back, thankful to be able to just nod and murmur yes, to keep him talking. They turned into the Walsh and she could see that at this part it was very wide. At one time the river had divided and now consisted of three channels, with grass and ti-trees rising from the two humps in its middle.

'That's where we swim,' Phil, one of her dancing partners of last night sitting on the front seat beside Yvonne, turned, smiling. 'And look, Deirdre, here's where we picnic. Just as good a place as your old coast can come up with, isn't it?'

She had to admit that it was, if in a different way, as she stepped on to a flat apron of ground covered with short green grass. From it the ground sloped gently down to the sandy river bed.

'It really is beautiful,' Deirdre thought as she

looked about her, and noted again the silence; for now that the cars had stopped the only sound was the noise which they themselves were making, and the rustle of swiftly running water.

'Come on, Deirdre.' Charles Wilson, who had joined the cavalcade on its journey to the picnic spot, caught hold of her hand. 'We're going swimming first, so be quick and change. We'll wait for you down at the pool.'

Deirdre managed to be reasonably quick, and only Norma, who never hurried, lagged behind. No one bothered with wraps, but Deirdre picked up her towelling robe and shrugged herself into its enveloping folds.

'Your turn, Deirdre!'

Undoing the buttons, she pulled her shirt away from her sore shoulders, and felt the ointment, cool and soothing, as Mrs. Liddle spread it carefully.

'I never thought of sunburn,' she confessed. 'We weren't in the blazing sun, not as we used to be at home on the beaches. It just didn't occur to me to put on sunburn cream.'

'But you were lying half in the sun under those trees when you were through swimming,' Mrs. Liddle reminded her. She looked again at Marge, whom she had anointed before she turned her attention to Deirdre, and clucked over her afresh. 'What a mess! Why don't you girls use a little sense? A fine picnic this is going to turn out for you if you start peeling tomorrow!'

No lobster was certainly ever any redder than Marge at that moment, and Deirdre was distinctly sore. But the picnic from the point of view of most of them had been a success, and now that it was over they were all very tired.

Deirdre was glad of the excuse that she was absolutely worn out. She slid down in her bed and pulled the sheet up to her ears, and she thought of all the things that had happened that day.

They had swum and dived, and played water polo with a beach ball, then climbed out of the river on to the bank to laze under the trees. That was where she had collected her sunburn. More cars arrived on the picnic scene, and a modest outing escalated into a full-scale family celebration. There were so many people to help with the food and the distribution of it that Deirdre and Norma unrepentantly disappeared while the preparations were at their height and sank down in the shade of some giant gums. Almost immediately a shadow fell across them, and Bill Darrell lowered himself to the vacant space beside Deirdre, while Tony dropped down in the vicinity of her friend.

There was a good deal of laughter and light conversation, and it lasted until some louder bursts of laughter reached them from a little group near to them. ... Bill Darrell referred to this rather noisy group as 'Blair and his harem'. It was certain that Blair was the centre of attention, and they were nearly all feminine.

Deirdre had been aware of this group all along. Like an antenna kept on a fixed line by a magnet her mind seemed to know at all times where that central figure was. She knew that he had changed out of his swim-suit and was dressed – not as the other men were, in shorts and sports shirts, but long trousers and a cream silk shirt. He was immaculate, as in fact he always was, and it actually drew a comment from Bill.

'Blair looks like a fashion plate,' he remarked. 'Extraordinary how he managed to keep so trim, isn't it, even under conditions like these?'

Deirdre looked at him rather closely.

'You like Blair, don't you, Bill?' she asked almost earnestly.

Bill smiled at her.

'Of course I do. Who doesn't? He's a wonderful bloke!'

'A lot of people appear to admire him, but do they all – approve of him?' she asked a little breathlessly.

Bill regarded her a trifle humorously.

'I'd say they do. I can't think of any reason why they shouldn't.' There was silence for a moment, and then he said: 'Perhaps you don't know about his leg? He spent six months of his youth on his back in hospital, with no one, doctor or family, knowing whether he would ever walk again. A tractor accident badly mangled his left leg, and it was more or less touch and go whether he'd be an invalid all his life. But Blair isn't the type who takes kindly to invalidism. A lot of people think he's arrogant. . . . But those months in hospital helped to make him so, and the determination that was necessary to put him on his feet again. He's proud of being a fit man today, and who can blame him?'

'Who, indeed?' Deirdre thought, feeling as if something inside her was actually wounded by the knowledge that Blair had once suffered so much.

Mrs. Payne called out at this juncture that the food was ready, and Bill and Tony left them to get supplies for the girls. Later they went for a walk along the bank of the creek, where the water-lilies in all their glory made a picture Deirdre knew she would never forget, and later still she collided with Blair for one brief moment, during which time he simply looked at her in an unsmiling way and said nothing. But apart from that one brief moment she had absolutely no contact with Blair while the picnic lasted, although she had plenty of other escorts, and she certainly couldn't complain that they ever left her alone for long.

It had been a long, exciting and rather tiring day, and now she was back in her own bed and dwelling on every separate incident that had made it quite a remarkable day.

And soon, despite a certain heaviness at heart, she fell asleep.

CHAPTER FOUR

THE Wilson farm was located on a flat, almost tree-less plain. There must be water somewhere about, Deirdre realized, but there was no outcrop of trees to mark a creek or a river. There were no clumps of greenery to break the monotony of the landscape, or to offer contrast and diversion to the eye.

As the truck in which she was travelling sped towards the farm buildings they looked to Deirdre more nearly as she had imagined farm buildings should be. Much wiser now than she had been when she arrived in that part of the world, she knew it was not true of the greater number of farms. But things here spoke of no lack of money, and of money well spent. Fences were new and well looked after. Paddocks were symmetical and already ploughed, deep furrow after deep furrow rolling away into the distance. But it was uninspiring, colourless, and everything that could be seen was useful rather than ornamental.

'I can read your mind,' Norma, who sat beside her in the truck, remarked, and proceeded to explain that the Wilsons were farmers pure and simple, and to them farming was a way of life and a way of making money. Large lawns and gardens, and even trees, did not figure in their scheme of things, but costly machinery did. Everything they had was of the very latest design, and for that reason labour-saving.

'I still think it would be nice to have a few trees,' Deirdre returned, as they came to a stop before a shed that was very like the one they had left at Brandts'. Mrs. Liddle had already alighted and was calling to them to get settled in.

'Slave-driver!' Edna responded, and Mrs. Liddle looked worried for a moment. But Edna was smiling at her, and the older woman was quite obviously relieved.

'I wouldn't like you to think I was that,' she said.

It was all so familiar by this time to Deirdre that walking into the big grading shed was like coming home. They settled in without loss of time, and it wasn't long before Deirdre's fingers were flying amongst the tobacco on the bench before her, but that didn't prevent her putting a question to Mrs. Liddle.

'Do we stay here long?' she asked her.

'Not long. And our next stop is Blair's. We'll be there longer.'

'How much longer?'

'We're usually there for a couple of months or more. He has three farms, actually, and there's a lot to be done. You could say we really work at Blair's. We'll be taking on an extra grader, too, a Mrs. Turley, the wife of the manager of one of Blair's farms.

And I don't mind telling you we need the help.'

A shadow darkened the doorway and Mr. Wilson came in accompanied by a small woman. Deirdre, who had met Charles's father, smiled now at his mother.

'So you're the girl Charles wants to help them win the tennis at Nerada this year,' she said, returning Deirdre's greeting. 'There doesn't seem to be much of you, my dear,' smiling. 'Perhaps it's as well he's been forbidden to make you practise.'

Deirdre stared. 'Oh no, did he really say that?' she exclaimed. 'I wouldn't dream of playing tournament tennis. I haven't played – except for a couple of week-ends here – for a long time now.'

'We knew that, of course,' Mr. Wilson now chimed in, 'but Charles was going to have you practise every evening after work, on the court out at the farm here.'

He glared at Mrs. Liddle as a sound of protest issued from her lips. 'All right, all right! I know you're behind, and if we'd taken this young lady here, I would have managed to arrange something to ensure that you lost no time. However . . .' he shrugged resignedly, 'it's too bad. I would have liked, myself, to come home victorious for once. Still, there it is. Come along, Mother,' he added, returning Mrs. Liddle's scowl with one as ferocious, 'we'd better get out of here. I must say, though, it's the outside of enough to receive such black looks in one's own grading shed.'

'Would you really have had to practise to play against Nerada, Deirdre?' Marge asked. 'You seemed to be playing all right to me on Sunday.'

Deirdre glanced at her in horror. 'Oh, Marge!' It was an exclamation. 'I'd be hit off the court by any reasonably competent A grade player in the condition I'm in now.' In a lighter tone, she went on, 'They seem to take their tennis seriously here; their supporters as well as their players.' She gave a gurgle of laughter as an exasperated look accompanied by a loud sigh came from the top of the other bench, and thereafter gave her attention entirely to the tobacco.

'I expect this is just how a cat must feel when it has had a saucer of cream and is waiting to have its back rubbed,' Deirdre remarked contentedly, as she lay in the shade with a cool breeze faintly stirring her hair. She stretched luxuriously, relaxing all her muscles, and yawned. 'How does one contrive a human purr?' she asked of Charles, as he dropped down beside her.

He shrugged, his mind, apparently, on other things.

'Care for a little exercise after work, Deirdre?' he asked. 'Not a game, but just knock a few balls back and forth.'

'I'd like that, Charles,' she answered. 'We could get in a good half-hour before dark. More than that, perhaps, if your mother wouldn't mind us being late for supper.'

'Oh, no, Deirdre,' he responded. 'No strenuous game. That sort of thing isn't allowed yet.'

She looked at him curiously. It was unlike him to avoid meeting her eyes.

'Tell, me, Charles,' she said a little anxiously, 'has the doctor said anything about me to Mrs. Liddle? She's developed rather an air of cherishing me lately, and I'd rather know. It isn't that I *mustn't* go in for much practice, is it?'

He shook his head.

'Of course not. At least—' And then the truth came out. 'As a matter of fact, I wanted to take you with us to Nerada next month, and put in some intensive practice, but when I spoke about it to Blair he flatly refused to allow you to accompany us. He not only refused, but said I had to discourage you from playing at all at the moment. Later on, perhaps, we might include you in the tournament, but not until you're very much better in health.'

Deirdre laughed aloud in her relief.

'Oh, but I'm very much better. And of course I'm going to play tennis with you, Charles,' she assured him gaily. 'Tournament tennis, if you think I'm up to it. Why shouldn't I? And it's nothing to do with Blair, in any case.'

'Oh, but it is,' he answered gravely. 'And if Blair says you're not to be included in the Nerada team you're not to be included.'

Her usually pale face flushed an angry red.

'That's nonsense,' she declared, in an angry tone. 'And you can tell Blair so if you like! Tell him I refuse to be cosseted by him or anyone else!'

Charles looked at her a little pityingly.

'Blair's right, you know,' he assured her, almost coaxingly. 'And in any case—'

'Yes?'

'Oh, nothing!'

'Will Lexia be included in the team?'

'She might be. Although if you come along—'

'There mightn't be room for the two of us!' She was quick to realize what he meant.

He rose with a shrug. 'I'm afraid you haven't any choice, Deirdre. I think we'll give playing a miss for tonight. We'll see what tomorrow brings.' He waved a casual hand as he walked away.

Seething, furious, she went inside to finish the afternoon's grading. The tobacco flew, keeping pace with her turbulent thoughts. She vowed to herself that she would go to Nerada, despite everything. And later that night, all during dinner and through the news broadcast afterwards which they always waited to hear, plans and counter-plans seethed through her mind. It was as if these latter had the power to conjure up phantoms, as glancing round from where she sat at the far end of the room with Norma, casually, indifferent to arrivals which were a matter of nightly occurrence here, she looked into eyes that danced as their owner formally greeted her. 'How are you, Deirdre? Are you settling in in your new place?'

'I'm very well, thank you,' she returned just as formally, and added meaningly, 'I've never felt better.'

'Good,' he nodded, his attention already given to his host.

She sat through the next half-hour, determined to tell him that whatever she did was her own business only, no one else's. The chance came when he went to collect some papers for their host from his parked car.

Slipping out of the side door, she went out to where he was rummaging in the glove box. He picked out the papers he wanted, turned, closing the car door.

'Well,' one eyebrow up, 'to what do I owe this pleasure, Miss Sheldon? Surely not my fatal charm?'

Deirdre felt her face burn. 'Please may I speak with you for a moment?'

'But certainly. Shall we go down to the far paddock? It's cosy and dark down there.' There was laughter in the low voice.

Even though he was mocking her, even though she knew he could trifle with her, and give no word of affection or explanation afterwards, the closeness of him beside her, the nearness of him, upset her. She clenched her hands suddenly, and came upright straight, her whole body rigid as she put deliberate dislike into her words. 'I would like to go to

71

Nerada to play tennis. No,' her hand went up as he made to speak, 'I don't mean with the top team, but there are other grades going and I play well enough for them. However, Charles says that you said I wasn't to play, therefore I shan't be picked.' She pushed into the background of her mind the knowledge that she hadn't particularly wanted to take part in the tournament until she had spoken to Charles that afternoon and indignation made her voice rise as she flung at him. 'You have no right to say what I will or will not do!'

'No,' the voice was mocking again, 'maybe I have no right, but I certainly have the power . . . and I'll use it too.'

'You won't!' She was angry now, past reasoning. 'Don't think you'll get away with this. I'll contrive some way of going. I can be as determined as you,' and she turned sharply away.

His voice, level, cold, with a harshness she had never before heard from that quarter, stopped her. 'You won't, you know, if I say no.' He continued in a different tone, 'This isn't personal, Deirdre. You should remember you have already have had a certain amount of – shall we say indisposition, resulting from carelessness.' His eyes travelled over her. She stood stiff, unyielding, as that all-embracing glance roved from head to toe, not hurrying, taking its time. 'You don't look bursting with health even now,' he remarked, letting his eyes swing up to meet hers, and as she raised a hand protestingly, he went on, 'I'll

72

make a bargain with you. I'll come out tomorrow and see how you make out, and then if we can arrange something to enable you not to overwork – well, we'll see.'

Unable to think of a crushing reply, she started for the quarters, but his voice, changed back to his normal low tones, again stopped her.

'One other condition, Deirdre.'

She swung back. 'Yes?'

'I know how difficult it is for you, but I won't have you saying Mr. Cameron – or for that matter, just nothing, or Hey you – in the presence of others. It's so unusual as to cause comment, and that I won't have. So when you absolutely have to call me something, could you manage "Blair"?' He waited for her reply.

'Very well, I will. Is there anything else?'

'Not unless you can bring yourself to say, "Is there anything else, Blair?" ' She heard his low chuckle follow her as she stalked away into the darkness.

Back safely in her own quarters she sat on the side of the bed, pummelling the pillow with her fists. 'He's intolerable,' she muttered, 'and I will go to Nerada despite what he says.' But she knew unerringly that his formidable 'You won't, you know' meant just that.

Hearing good nights called as the others left the house, she hurriedly changed and slipped into bed. Norma put her head round the curtain, but eyeing the motionless figure she let the drapery drop and

73

went quietly away.

The next day felt a million years long to Deirdre. She was restless, wondering if Blair really was going to keep his word. However, in the afternoon tea break Mr. Wilson turned up at the shed, spoke to Mrs. Liddle. He walked then to where Deirdre was lounging against one of the uprights.

'Well, Deirdre,' he began, 'what do you say to having a game with Charles this evening? I'll work in your place for the last half-hour. That will give you quite a bit of daylight. I don't expect I'll grade as much tobacco as you would, but we'll make it up to you.'

'Oh, Mr. Wilson, as if I wanted it made up to me! Thank you for helping out. Anyway, I'm doing all right. In fact,' she beamed at him, 'I didn't know I could earn so much money.'

He rose awkwardly, patted her shoulder. His 'You'll do, Deirdre,' gave her a warm feling of belonging.

Instead of dragging the next few hours fled. Deirdre went over to the quarters and pulled on shorts instead of her skirt, socks and tennis shoes. She had no time to bath and change, and in any case would have to shower after tennis, so she just shrugged at her dirt and decided she would have to do. Reaching for her racquet, she drew a deep breath and made her way to the court.

When still a few hundred yards away she saw the familiar battleship grey car, and walked more slowly. Both men turned to face her, and the taller one asked: 'Are you ready to take Charles on, Deirdre?'

She could only nod and walk to the receiving end of the court. He's different today, she reflected in some confusion. Dressed in khaki shorts and shirt, immaculate, stiffly starched and shining with cleanliness, he appeared more as other men, and as approachable. She recalled her disparagement of his dress on the day of the picnic, and then Charles was serving, and for the next half-hour she had no thought at all except for the ping of the ball and her own efforts to send it back. Imperceptibly, from merely hitting them back and forth, Charles began to place them. It was then that she found out how out of practice she really was.

Hearing voices on the sideline, she was aware that it must be after knocking-off time, and wondered how on earth she could manage to last the hour out when suddenly Charles caught the balls and dropped them at the base line. Blair had come out on to the court.

'Enough for now, Deirdre,' and there was a crispness unusual in the soft voice. 'Charles is going to give Norma a hit. Yes, you are,' he repeated, as a protest became audible. 'You're our reserve, Norma, and if we don't want you, the B grade does.'

As Norma came on without further argument, Mrs. Liddle commented dryly, 'It's nice to be you, Blair. Just decree something and have it obeyed right away!'

He laughed, both at her and at Norma, and remarked to no one in particular: 'But the secret is to order only something you really want done, and then enforce it. Isn't that so, Norma?' He gave her a tiny smack with a racquet as she passed him. 'Get out there and give us some action,' he added.

Deirdre had walked off slowly and leant her racquet down by the wire netting fence. She was trembling and her knees felt as if they were made of a particularly yielding rubber. A hand was suddenly under her elbow.

'Over here, Deirdre. I have an old friend waiting for you.' She went over to the seat with Blair's fingers holding her arm.

Aware of nothing but the hand holding her, she wondered hazily who could be there. Then a big white cardigan was draped around her shoulders and her eyes fell away from the remembrance in those glinting blue ones above her.

'Thank you. You were right, of course.' The apology came a little breathlessly. She waited for his 'I told you so', knowing now, herself, that she was in no condition to play. But when he did speak his voice was dispassionate, matter-of-fact.

'You couldn't expect to be anything else but exhausted after that workout. Charles didn't pull any punches. We'll see how you do tomorrow.'

Deirdre hugged the sweater to her. Suddenly she felt extraordinarily lighthearted and happy. The evening around her was merging into night. The overhead arch of lapis lazuli was giving way to a wash of warm orange turning to the palest lavender as the sun slipped even lower to vanish as they were talking. A breeze sighed its way across the court. Abruptly, Blair was standing, pulling her with him. 'Shower now, Deirdre, and rub yourself down thoroughly,' he ordered. 'I'll see you tomorrow.'

Her mouth still open at his issuing of such a personal command, she turned obediently towards their quarters. His voice following stopped her for a moment. 'Keep that old friend, Deirdre, until the season is over.'

Vigorously towelling after her shower, she thought only that Blair had said she hadn't done too badly with the workout. Even so, she was astonished at how understanding he had been – not arrogant, or what was worse, mocking. However, honesty compelled her to add that he had been proved right. He had had no need to be anything else but pleasant.

Stepping from the shower, she bumped into the others returning from the courts. A glance at Norma and a big grin spread across her face.

'I've left the shower vacant for you, Norma,' she told her with spurious sympathy. 'Would you care for some assistance to get there?'

'Not you too, Deirdre! I expected such an attitude from these – these . . .' she flung out a hand, 'but you! I thought you were my friend!'

'Was it so bad?'

'That damned Blair!' This time there was real, not imitation, indignation in her voice. 'He just simply hasn't the *right* to do the things he does!' What else she had been about to say was lost, drowned in a shout of laughter.

'It's all right for you,' she continued to them all, when she could be heard. 'You weren't on the receiving end. Just you wait,' she threatened. 'I'll think of some way of getting even with him!'

'I wish you joy of it, Norma,' Mrs. Liddle told her dryly, and marched into the quarters.

CHAPTER FIVE

It really is like laughter, brazen, raucous laughter, Deirdre reflected drowsily, hearing the laughing jackasses performing their usual morning chorus. She opened one eye to see how late it was, and to know if she could have a few more minutes snuggled under the bedclothes. The kookaburras always began their serenade at daybreak when the sun's first rays slanted into the pale half light of the coming dawn, and it was an added source of delight up here to be awakened every morning by them. As she swung her feet over the side of the bed a groan came softly to her lips. For a moment she had forgotten yesterday, but now every aching muscle in her body brought back the memory. She glanced down at the cardigan she had folded and placed on a chair beside her bed. Reaching out, she took it up, holding it to her face. It still smelt faintly of that elusive perfume; bringing oh, so vividly to her mind the memory of its owner . . . the feel of his arms . . . abruptly she dropped it back, and turning picked up her towel and sponge-bag.

Someone called to her.

'Deirdre, you're wanted on the phone!'

She looked blankly at the younger Wilson boy as he came into the shed with the message. 'Are you sure it's for me, David?' she inquired in surprise. No one but Charles had ever rung her up, up here in Limberg, and that was only for tennis.

He grinned cheekily at her. 'If your name is Deirdre, with no surname, I expect it is. That's the one they asked for.'

'Oh well,' laying down a handful of tobacco, she followed him across to the house. The answer to her 'Hello' made her breath catch. It was the last voice she expected to hear.

'How are the muscles this morning, Deirdre?'

'Getting better now, thank you,' she answered a trifle breathlessly.

'That's good. I thought I'd find out if you were still capable of another go this afternoon. Who knows, I might even give you some practice myself.'

'Oh no . . . no!' At the open horror in her tone, his soft chuckle came back clearly.

'Well, you'll always have that to look forward to. I'll see you later,' and she heard the click as he put down the phone.

She laid her own receiver back gently, then drew a deep breath and walked out to the kitchen to thank Mrs. Wilson.

Marge was the first to break the silence after her return to the grading shed. 'It's not supposed to be good manners to ask, I know, Deirdre,' she burst out irrepressibly, 'but was it about something nice?'

Willing only mild interest into her expression for

she actually, literally, could not bring herself to discuss Blair, Deidre anwered: 'Oh, the phone call. One of the men I've met here about the training for tennis yesterday ...' her voice trailed off, then resumed. 'How on earth could anyone have heard so soon ... ?' she crossed her fingers guiltily behind her back.

Mrs. Liddle went to get more tobacco, and work proceeded as usual. Tennis was Tennis up here; everyone was interested.

At five o'clock Deirdre went over to the court. Blair was winding the net and greeted her with a nod only, before walking out to adjust the height. The game went on and she was again beginning to think that she could not last a moment longer when Charles caught both balls and came up to the net. Grinning into her hot face, he told her complacently, 'Blair says that's enough for today, Deirdre. Do you agree?' His grin grew wider at her indignant look.

'We played longer than we did yesterday, if that's any consolation to you,' he said, adding, 'Here's Norma and Tony to take over.'

Deirdre looked the surprise she felt, but they were both indeed coming on to the court.

'Doesn't Charles make you run enough, Norma?' she inquired softly, and caught the flash of white teeth from Tony as he passed. She watched for a few minutes, then excused herself to go home and shower. Blair had left when she returned.

The days fell into a pattern – work; the usual tea breaks, and the extra ones when visitors arrived, and it was astonishing how many visitors did arrive to talk tennis, until Mrs. Liddle put her foot firmly down: then tennis and more tennis. Deirdre felt that her play was back to normal now; she was going the full hour with Charles, and occasionally giving him something he couldn't handle.

Suddenly it wanted only a week to the tournament, and as she sat watching from the sidelines after her own workout, she wondered when she would see Blair again; he had not been present since the second day she had begun to practise. Observing Mrs. Liddle about to leave, she rose and walked beside her to the quarters. She had come to feel a real affection for this abrupt, caustic woman; and at least, while talking to her, no sudden happening, no unexpected abrupt flash of even an everyday occurrence brought an image, vivid, vibrant, before her eyes, to shatter the cocoon of indifference with which she tried to enwrap herself. If only she could forget there was such a person as Blair. It wasn't much to ask, she often thought, but then. . . .

She smiled, parting with Mrs. Liddle, and went quickly to the annex. She showered and donned a pretty afternoon frock, instead of the more usual cotton dress which they normally wore in the evenings. Charles had asked some of the crowd to stay, and others were coming in after dinner.

And after that same dinner, as her partner swung

her around in the last violent pivot, she decided that her tennis practice had been an easier task. Jiving, the way Phil did it, was no gracious minuet. Deirdre, who had never before in her life jived, had just been initiated into some of the more simple steps. Her partner bowed from the waist and proffered his arm. Placing the tips of her fingers on its extreme edge, she giggled helplessly at the contrast of the exaggeratedly polished bow with the dance they had just finished. Still, it was fun to be young and silly occasionally; and they were certainly being silly tonight. So many had stayed to eat that two long tables had had to be joined together. Everyone had set to and washed up afterwards and then got ready the party fare. Deirdre had mixed hard-boiled eggs, sliced ham and tongue taken from the fridge, and pressed a stronger hand than hers into the opening of tins of asparagus and salmon.

It really hadn't started out as a party. A few more men had dropped in to watch the tennis, Charles had phoned some girls; and here they were.

Deirdre directed her steps to the end of the cement veranda on which they were dancing, but Phil, who was more one of Marge's set, dashing, spoilt, given too much too quickly, although harmless in Deirdre's opinion, turned his towards the open. He stopped and grinned at her.

'Oh no, Phil.' She returned the grin quite amiably but continued nevertheless on her own way.

'Have a heart, Deirdre. You know you've never

before seen tobacco growing in the moonlight. Just look at that moon!'

'Yes, isn't it wonderful, Phil; and you know, I'm not as green as all that. I wouldn't be here if the tobacco was still growing.'

'But, Deirdre, there are the trees and paddocks. They all look marvellous by moonlight.'

'I don't doubt it in the least, Phil. This way.' It was said firmly, and, knowing he was beaten, he laughed, not at all put out, piloting her towards the group on the edge of the veranda. 'You can't blame a bloke for trying, Deirdre,' was all he vouchsafed.

She slid down in a deck chair beside Norma, who had not been dancing at all, and who invariably said when asked, 'You couldn't expect me to dance. Why, I've had to do all Deirdre's work as well as my own today! She has been resting up to save all *her* energy for tennis!'

Phil flung himself down on to the grass on the outside of them. She lay back and gazed at the moonlight. As Phil had said, it was a beautiful night, brilliant white light causing the shadows to stand out, stark and clear, ebony and silver. Deirdre stirred restlessly, and gladly brought her attention back to the more normal atmosphere of the party as Norma straightened out of her lounging position. A late car had pulled up and she saw her companion relax as two men stepped out and walked towards their hostess. She watched as they picked their way over outstretched feet down the veranda after having spoken with Mrs. Wilson. Tony gave a grave good night to everyone and turning to Norma, held out his hand. She rose and walked into his arms.

Deirdre felt tears sting her eyelids as she watched them dance along the polished cement floor. There was a oneness about them, an intangible something that could be sensed. The man did not hold her close, or dance cheek to cheek. It was a much deeper thing. Her eyes followed them wistfully. It was something to know one was beloved even if it was not all smooth sailing for them, she reflected enviously.

From the seat into which he had dropped as Norma went to dance, Bill Darrell's eyes followed her gaze. 'They make a nice couple, Deirdre,' he said gently. 'It's to be hoped things go right for them.'

'But, Bill, in these days people marry whom they please.' There was bewilderment in her voice. 'And Tony is as modern as any man I know,' she went on. 'He doesn't talk much, I grant you, but I would expect him to know his own mind very well. There's nothing weak about him.'

'As you say, Deirdre. Still, he would have a strong loyalty to his family. And Italian parents like to have a hand in their children's marriages, you know. However, they both know how to wait, and with an attraction such as theirs . . .' He leant back, closing his eyes. Glancing at him, she thought how tired he looked.

He went on slowly, his eyes still closed, 'I should be up dancing with you, Deirdre. Tell me what a bad companion I am and I'll make an effort.'

'You'll lie back and rest if that's how you feel, Bill. Anyhow, I've been jiving with these wild Indians since dinner. I deserve a rest too.'

They sat together in companionable silence, and as the music finished Mr. Wilson walked out with a tray full of brimming glasses. 'Only for the grown-ups,' he remarked, handing Bill one. 'Yours is coming up now, Deirdre,' he added. Charles had appeared behind him with tall frosted lemon and orange drinks clinking with ice.

'Why aren't you at Lexia's, Bill?' Charles inquired, taking the last drink from his tray and dropping down beside Phil on the grass. 'The parents should be there, but with that bad elbow of Dad's, he thought he'd be better off home.' Charles laughed. 'And then we go and get up our own party.'

'Boy, and is it some party at Lexia's!' Phil chimed in. 'All the fixings – exotic food brought up from the coast, floodlights in the grounds, music specially imported from Nerada. I should know, I had to get my own lunch or go hungry. My mother has been over there all day, helping.'

'Actually, you made up for it at dinner time,' Marge put in. 'I was watching you, and really, Phil, wondering where on earth you could possibly be storing it all,' she grinned cheekily down at him.

A smile playing about Tony's lips caught Deirdre's eye. Wanting to hear more of this affair at Lexia's, she asked him, 'You seem amused, Tony. Why aren't you there? I mean, I can't understand why only some members of a family are going and others not invited.'

His smile became broader as he glanced Bill's way. 'Actually, Deirdre,' he told her, 'we owe Bill's appearance here tonight to Lexia. I happened merely to be present when she invited him to this do of hers. Blair was standing there by her side. Bill looked at him, received no help whatsoever, then at me, and said brazenly, "I'm sorry, Lexia, but I'm promised to Tony for the night. We're going to Nerada." And because Bill is always truthful, to Nerada we've been.' He smiled again at the chuckles which swept the circle.

'Did you really go, Tony? All that way?'

Tony glanced across at Bill and answered gravely, 'Of course we did. That's why we're late. And all the time,' he added, his smile becoming wider as he remembered, 'Blair stood there by Lexia, saying not a word, that wicked grin of his glued to his face; you know ...?' Tony looked round for confirmation, and received nods from everyone present. 'Then when Lexia had finished with Bill here, Blair gave one glance at me ... me, mind you, the innocent party, saying in that soft voice of his, "Enjoy yourself, and as you're going to Nerada you might do an errand for me. I'll ring you!" And he did. Ring me, I mean. So there we were.'

'Couldn't you make some excuse, Tony?' one of the men exclaimed. 'I mean, it's a damn long way to go, thirty miles there and another thirty back for nothing, and . . .'

'Oh no!' In shocked accents Tony interrupted him. 'We'd said we were going, and as far as I was concerned, and as far as Bill was concerned too, and much more certainly as far as Blair was concerned, that was that.'

'I expect it's about supper-time,' Mrs. Wilson remarked into the small silence which had fallen as everyone digested this. She got up from her chair and the girls rose to follow behind. Edna was dancing a tango with Stan. They had the veranda to themselves, and looking at them as she passed, Deirdre thought how effortless the intricate steps appeared when done by experts.

Finishing her share of the chores, Deirdre took her cup of tea and made her way back to Bill's side. Glancing at the two heaped plates on either side of his canvas chair, she laughed. 'I'll make a bet that you never get through all that,' she told him gaily.

The smile she received in return was lazy, warm. 'As Marge went to a great deal of trouble to find my favourite provender, I'll have to make a darn good try.'

Under cover of the softly playing radiogram,

and the loud hum of conversation, Deirdre asked carelessly, 'Will it be a marvellous party at Lexia's tonight, Bill? And didn't you really want to go?'

He finished some asparagus and wiped his fingers on a paper napkin. 'It will be a very dull affair, I expect, Deirdre. Some officials from the Government are up here on a water survey. They've been staying with Blair, and Lexia wanted to give this reception for them.' He smiled his lazy smile at her again, asked quizzically, 'Does that answer your first question? Here's an answer for your second. No, I really didn't want to go. Blair knew that. He knows most things that happen in his bailiwick – everything – that could touch his way of life in particular. It didn't matter to him at all, my not going, but he couldn't control that devilish sense of humour of his.'

Deirdre couldn't stop the next question, even though she had not meant to ask it. But this was Bill, to whom she could say anything.

'She is lovely, isn't she, Bill? And she has everything working for her! Looks, figure, and all the money she could ever use!'

Bill didn't ask about whom she was speaking. He merely replied, 'But she hasn't kindness or compassion, Deirdre; or generosity and the art of giving, and you needn't worry about her.' He touched briefly the hand that held the neglected cup of tea in her lap, and rose before she could question him further. 'Excuse me now, Deirdre. I must speak with my hostess. I have to be going if I can get Tony away.'

In bed, after the lights of the last car had swung down the road and she had helped carry plates and empty ashtrays, Deirdre could at last give her attention to Bill's final remark. She lay, her face to the window, trying to remember every nuance of his voice as he had spoken to her, and recollected only that he had told her not to worry. She turned over and put an arm across her eyes. Well, she would take his advice. There was Nerada and the tournament in the offing.

CHAPTER SIX

CHARLES came through the doorway of the big shed and perched on the corner of a bench. 'I think,' he remarked casually, with an all-embracing glance, 'I'll let you off tennis for this evening.'

'Why?' The word came curtly from Norma. She knew there must be something behind that smug look which accompanied the lordly offer.

'Because, my dear, you and I, with Deirdre, are going places – to Lexia's, no less. So put on your best bibs and tuckers, and I'll even borrow Dad's car, instead of taking my old jalopy, to enable you to arrive in style.' He gave an airy wave as he hopped off the bench and went out whistling.

Deirdre felt as if she were at school again and was waiting for an interview with the headmistress over some misdemeanour she had committed, when later that evening Charles turned his father's car off the main road and its powerful headlights outlined the trees paralleling the side lane which led to Lexia's farm. She deliberately, for courage, placed her hand in the crook of Charles's arm as she walked by his side up the two wide steps on to the dazzling, brightly lighted, flower-decked patio.

'You know these people, don't you?' Lexia welcomed them as they reached her, and with a casual wave of her hand at the scattered groups she drifted away to greet some new arrivals.

'It's as well we do,' Charles drawled in the tone normal to his voice when around Lexia, and in the moment before she was surrounded, Deirdre wondered why he disliked their hostess so much; and then stopped wondering about anything as a car came swiftly along the dirt road. Knowing that Blair was not present, she gave it a fleeting side-glance and saw him helping one of the elder women tennis players from its interior.

'It's my fault we're late,' this worthy began breathlessly as they mounted the steps. 'One of my infants just wouldn't go to bed. You can thank Blair we're here at last.'

'I expect the price was a bit high, though,' he made answer, laughter sounding through his words. 'I think ... mind you, I only *think* that she manoeuvred out of me a promise to maybe marry her when she grew up. How old is she, Mrs. Malcombe?' he added, taking no notice whatever of the ribald remarks cast his way. 'Nine ... um? In ten years' time she'll be just the right age, won't she?' His gaze had fastened on Deirdre as he said this, eyes glinting, wicked, holding hers for a full half minute before he turned to Lexia.

Utterly taken aback by that brazen, impudent look, Deirdre watched him as he was claimed by two committee members. Tonight she thought he could have been taken for a pattern of a pirate from the Middle Ages – swashbuckling, arrogant, and oh, so sure of himself! She could also understand now the remark Tony had made about him when talking of the Nerada episode, and knew why everyone had concurred without the slightest question . . . wicked was certainly the word for it! She wondered, knowing by now a little of his ways, what he had been – or maybe was – up to.

Lexia's voice cut through the hum of conversation. 'Shall we go inside and get this business over?' she suggested, leading the way into the lounge. It was huge, modern as a glossy magazine spread, flowers everywhere, but, Deirdre noticed, no books lying around, none at all.

The secretary rapped at a small table placed there for his convenience and began, 'As you know we are here to finalize the arrangements for the week-end. I have the lists that the captain,' he glanced at Blair, 'and the selectors have made out.' He hesitated, coughed, and sent an imploring look in Blair's direction. Deirdre wondered what was coming. Secretaries as a rule – and this was something she did know about – mostly went calmly about their business, did as their committee told them, and didn't bother to apologize to anyone.

'This year,' he was saying as she brought her attention back to the meeting, 'they have decided to change things around a little. You will agree, I think, that tennis is tennis, whether we win or lose, and our Nerada friends give us a wonderful time irrespective of how we play. But we thought, after a comprehensive discussion by all the committee, that with some reallocation we might actually give them a run for their money this time. Well,' abruptly the voice went crisp, 'here are the lists. We've changed all grades around and hope for everyone's co-operation.'

'Number one pair are Blair and Deirdre.' Deirdre came upright with a jolt, Lexia's lips thinned to a white line, everyone began to talk at once. Blair sat carelessly sideways, doodling with a pencil on what looked like the back of an old envelope. Watching that hand, her eyes downcast, Deirdre thought again how little like a farmer's hard-working hand it was. She wondered, too, if it really came to pass, how she would manage to play for two whole days with him and not let him see how much she. . . . She drew in her breath sharply, and blindly brought her mind back to the happenings in the room.

Lexia had regained her composure. Her voice cut coldly through the swell of sound. 'I don't think I would care to play with anyone else but Blair; in fact, I don't think that I could.' The threat implicit in her voice was recognized by all.

The secretary shrugged, dropped his papers and resumed his seat, clearly putting any responsibility on to other shoulders.

Then Blair spoke, and Deirdre thought with a

pang how different he sounded – not a trace of the mockery he used to her, none of the laughter she always associated with him. He spoke gravely, a little coaxingly. 'Don't you really think you could, Lexia? I'm sure you could do most things you wanted to do. It's too late now to rearrange the teams, you know.' No latent threat this, merely a statement of plain facts.

A quick glance about the circle of faces caused Lexia to hesitate a moment, then abruptly she made her decision. 'All right then, Blair. But don't blame me if I don't play as well with Charles,' she shrugged, turning away.

Unable to eat supper, sitting silent amid the buzz of conversation flying all around her, thankful for the cup of tea to give her attention to, Deirdre had to apologize as Charles leant closer and spoke for the second time.

'I'm sorry, Charles. What was it you said?'

'I said you'd better play as if your life depended on it, after all this.'

'I just don't know how I'll play, Charles,' she answered uncertainly. 'I expected to be playing with you, or Tony. I'll never play with Blair. I'll be petrified. Did you know about this before we came here?'

'Well, I had an idea; but it wasn't official. Also, Lexia needn't think I'm crying for joy at having to play with her, because I'm not.' He grinned suddenly, said very softly, 'She hadn't a hope of getting things changed. If it had been merely the selectors, she might have swung it. However, it was Blair himself who suggested the change-round; and she might just as well have tried shifting a brick wall. She would have had as much chance.'

Deirdre shivered. This information gave to Blair a different aspect altogether, and she wasn't sure if she cared for it.

Turning off the main road into their own familiar gravel lane, Charles suddenly broke the silence that had reigned in the car the whole way home. He slowed, pushed his head out of the window, and looked anxiously up at the sky.

'I think we're going to get some rain,' he sounded glum. 'I hope it comes now and not at the week-end.'

'Oh, Charles, for heaven's sake! Just relax and enjoy your tennis. You make such heavy weather of only a week-end's sport.' There was a seldom used edge to Deirdre's voice.

'Don't you care at all, Deirdre?' he demanded.

'No, I don't. It doesn't worry me one way or another. I play as well as I can. If I win I'm happy about it, if not, there's always another day. Thank you,' she added as he pulled up to let them out, and then, 'Sorry I was abrupt,' she told him, and waved as she turned away.

She woke later that night and heard the sound so often heard at home in the wet season; but which she had as yet not experienced up here in the north. The soft drumming on the roof was a lullaby. A smile crossed her face as she sank deeper into the pillows. Poor Charles!

It was still raining when they started work, heavy, persistent rain. Charles came over around ten o'clock to say gloomily that he had rung Nerada and they said that it was raining there, too. He looked offended when they laughed at him, and stalked away in high dudgeon at Mrs. Liddle's laconic, 'It's only Thursday, Charles. Go away and let us work.'

The rain continued all day, and all night too. However, by the next morning it had degenerated into a steady drizzle. Charles was actually smiling when they saw him, and called cheerfully from across the tractor he was working on, 'I think we'll be lucky, it should clear today.' And indeed, clear it did. By late afternoon the sun was doing its best to shine through what clouds were left.

Dinner was a hilarious meal. Charles was threatened with no transport if he didn't quieten down a bit, but as he knew the threat was an idle one, it was no wonder it didn't succeed. Nevertheless, there was no dawdling when the meal was finished. They went directly to their quarters, and in a few minutes all lights were out.

Deirdre woke next morning with that feeling one has when, subconsciously, one knows that something importantly different is about to happen. Her gaze went swiftly to the window, but only blue sky was visible. It came again, the noise which had awakened her. She grinned. Charles was revving up the car engine, calling out, and doing his ardent best to wake everyone in the vicinity.

She lay quietly for a few moments, her mind busy with thoughts of the coming week-end; however, deciding to meet it minute by minute as it came along, she resolutely thrust all misgivings aside and slipped out of bed.

A scene of violent activity met them when Charles braked to a halt in front of the hotel. Only eight cars were officially going, but considerably more than that were already present as they drew in to called greetings and the honking of horns. Even more were parked outside houses at varied parts of the small township, and Deirdre could see luggage boots, mouth agape, swallowing the provender being stowed carefully, or thrust higgledy-piggledy, according to its owner's disposition, into their various maws. She smiled to herself. For a mere tennis tournament, they were certainly making a gala event out of it!

Making his way through the group of surrounding cars, Henry accosted her, saying, 'You're to come with us, Deirdre. Charles's load is made up. Here, sit with Bill and Yvonne, and please stay put,' he pleaded. 'I have orders to look after you, but I have to collect some things first.' He was hurrying away even as the words came from over his shoulder.

'Only look at the confusion! Will we ever get away?' Deirdre laughed at the question, but nevertheless she wondered.

Bill, however, had no such doubts. 'In ten minutes or less, Deirdre,' he told her. 'Just relax and enjoy yourself.' And, incredible as it seemed, in less than Bill's ten minutes all semblance of disorder had disappeared and the cavalcade of cars was running swiftly along the wide paved road. And, she thought, swiftly was the operative word! Distance had no meaning for these young farmers. They were used to driving to Nerada, and even to Cairns, much as city-dwellers dressed and drove into town.

In an amazingly short time they were entering Nerada's main street. Only having seen it previously from the train window, Deirdre gazed about her with interest. A new hotel in the course of construction was standing silent and empty today, surrounded by its scaffolding. The blank windows and unfinished brick walls boldly outlined against the vast blue arch overhead. Another, seemingly wholly comprised of glass and aluminium, could proudly have taken its place on the Gold Coast. She remarked on all the new buildings, and Henry chimed in from the back seat.

'It was different when we first came, Bill, wasn't it? But tobacco has changed all that. It's king now. Here's hoping it stays that way for a long time!'

99

'Amen,' she heard Bill murmur, as he drew into the kerb before a hotel. It wasn't one of the glass brick affairs, but an older edifice with a wide over-hung veranda of the old style. She saw that Blair had parked his car in the shade which was provided by a magnificent avenue of trees growing the whole length of the street, and watched as he helped his passengers to alight. She wasn't surprised, either, to note that Lexia was among them.

'As soon as we've been allotted our rooms, let's go shopping,' Norma suggested as they waited amid the flurry of welcome going on all about them. 'There are a dozen things I need that we can't buy at home.'

'Me too,' exclaimed Marge, coming up to join them. She had travelled with Mrs. Liddle, of whom Henry had said: 'Why, of course she had to come along; there can be no show without Punch.'

Deirdre felt a hand come under her elbow and experienced the familiar butterflies in the region of her tummy. Blair guided the three girls into the hotel and up the stairs.

'As you're a newcomer here, Deirdre, I've ar-ranged for them to put you and Norma together.' His voice held a crispness which was unusual, as he continued, 'They look after us very well as we always stay here. You should be quite comfortable.' They had rounded the corner at the top of the stair-way and he released the arm which had remained under his fingers, but oh, so rigidly. She reached across and covered with her other hand the place where those fingers had rested. Although gone themselves, the mark of their imprint remained.

'Here we are.' He had paused at the first doorway. 'Henry is bringing up both your cases; or he was,' he corrected himself dryly, as more than one pair of heavy footsteps were heard climbing the stairs. Henry was certainly coming up the steps, but it was Tony who carried the two suitcases.

Blair raised one brow, and his teeth flashed white as he took in the loaded figure. Tony's teeth, no less white in only a slightly darker face, returned the mocking smile calmly. Depositing the bags inside the room, he remained standing silently by the door. Blair's glance took in the room thoroughly – like a manager seeing that everything was in order, reflected Deirdre, sternly repressing a desire to giggle at this unexpected side of him. Apparently satisfied, he spoke, this time in his habitual low tone, and she wondered what had happened to make him speak as he had a short time ago. Used as she now was to his way of behaviour, she could mark his moods by the inflection in his speech. She knew that he had forgotten his previous irritation as he asked them, speaking more to Norma than to her, 'What do you propose to do before lunch? Are you going shopping? You'll be working for me next week, you know, so if you see anything extra you need, you can always get an advance.'

Norma looked shocked, horrified. 'I can just see

Mrs. Liddle's face!' she exclaimed. 'No ... no, thank you, Blair. We have plenty.' She crossed the room and went out with Tony.

'And naturally you have plenty too, Deirdre?' There was mockery now. She could only nod. He appeared to her to fill the whole room as he stood there, and she was unable to follow Norma as he was blocking the doorway. Making no effort to move from it, he considered her thoughtfully.

'Well, no matter,' he said at last. 'I can see Mrs. Liddle.'

'But, truly, I do have plenty,' she assured him. 'We hardly spend money up here, and as I've remarked before, I didn't realize I could earn so much. Why, I might even be able to ...' She broke off abruptly.

'You might even be able to do what, Deirdre?' he prompted her as she remained silent.

'I was just thinking aloud. May I get through to Norma, please, Blair?' She was unconscious of the entreaty in her voice.

'In a moment. What may you be able to do?' Knowing him by now, and that tone, she answered flatly, 'I've always wanted to be a teacher. If I had money to keep me while I studied, I could possibly train in Brisbane. And,' her head went up, defiantly she straightened to her whole five feet two, 'I could make a career out of it, not merely put in time as I'm now doing.'

He was smiling again, his eyes filled with that

expression she disliked so intensely, as he answered.

'I don't think that will be necessary. I really don't think you have any chance of getting away from us. I even expect there'll be a few offers floating round to enable you to stay.' An edge crept into his voice as he took in the faint colour staining her face, and he added, 'It looks, too, as if the offers might have already began, but we'll surely arrange something. We simply can't afford to lose a tennis player of your calibre, you know.' With that patronizing finish, he stood aside to allow her to precede him through the open doorway.

Norma was talking to Tony at the balcony railing. She turned as they came out. One glance at Deirdre's face and she swiftly crossed the space between them to slip her hand through the younger girl's arm.

'Ready now, Deirdre?' It was Deirdre to whom she spoke, but it was on the tall figure who had emerged by her side that Norma's challenging gaze was fixed.

Blair returned the look, then laughed. 'I'm afraid you're out of your class, Norma,' he said softly. 'I'm far beyond your league. Still ...' he touched her cheek lightly with the back of his fingers as he passed them both to go down the stairs.

'I'll see you later,' Tony, following him, cast over his shoulder.

Deirdre drew a deep, deep breath. Her lungs felt

empty, airless. She too turned resolutely in the direction of the steps. 'We'd better get this shopping done, I expect, if we're to be ready on time,' was all she could think to say.

A couple of pairs of white socks clutched in her hand, Deirdre smiled at the busy assistant and waited for some attention, handed over money in exchange for the small package when her turn came, and then took a firm hold of Norma's arm, exclaiming, 'Now lead me to a good café. I want to buy some chocolates for Mrs. Liddle.'

Knocking into them as she hurried past in the crowded aisle, a young girl gave them a casual smile of apology, then came to a sudden stop, smiling widely at Norma. 'This is Mary Hallam, Deirdre,' Norma introduced her, returning the smile with warmth. 'She plays against us; also, she has two big beautiful brothers, so cultivate her. Deirdre Sheldon, Mary, who is grading with us this year, and moreover, is playing for Lim this week-end,' she added.

There was a pucker of concentration between the Nerada girl's eyes. However, she only said 'How do you do' pleasantly, before asking for all the Limberg news.

'Do you know, Deirdre,' she remarked as she was saying good-bye, 'your face seems familiar, but I can't place it. I haven't met you before, have I?'

'I shouldn't think so. I don't belong up here. I'm from Cairns,' Deirdre told her.

'Oh, in that case . . .' Mary turned back to Norma and Deirdre walked ahead with Marge. An exclamation from behind caused her to swing back.

'Sheldon! Why, of course! You're the girl we saw playing tennis in Cairns last year.' She scrutinized Deirdre more carefully. 'You look different. But then we only saw you on the court.' A thought seemed to strike her. 'On number one court, too! Why, you were playing in the finals of the Championships. Well!'

'We didn't win, you know,' came quietly from Deirdre.

'You might not have, but it was dashed good tennis all the same. Who are you playing with this week-end?'

As Deirdre made no effort to answer, Norma replied for her. 'Blair, of course.'

'Oh . . . oh!' Mary gave a gurgle of real enjoyment. 'What price Lim this week-end? This . . . this I must certainly go and spread around. See you this afternoon!' She was off with a gay wave of her hand.

Their shopping finished, the girls strolled back to the hotel, through less crowded streets now that the shops were closing. Busy with the thoughts of her former life which the encounter with Mary had aroused Deirdre knew with certainty that she would never return to it. She would do what she had told Blair she was going to do, such a short time ago; try to find a permanent niche for herself. Her reverie was terminated as they passed from the dense shade of the tree-lined avenue into the brilliant sunshine, by a command from the balcony high above their heads telling them in no uncertain terms to get a move on.

Charles and Tony waited for them just inside the dining-room door, and escorted them to a large centre table. Deirdre heard Blair's soft voice from across the room, though not the words themselves. He was seated at a corner table with Lexia and a girl whom Deirdre did not know, and who was as dark as Lexia was fair, and as beautiful. She noticed, too, with surprise, that the fourth occupant of the table was Bill Darrell. Knowing how close he and Blair were, that gave no cause for comment. However, Bill also made no secret of his ... not dislike; that was too strong a word; his distaste for Lexia.

Returning from her shower, Deirdre found Norma ready and waiting for her, and hurriedly slipped into her dress, Norma zipping it up for her. She applied a darker and deeper lipstick than she normally used, and was rather more generous with it than was her usual practice, as protection against the sun, and then, finally dressed, pivoted before the mirror for her own inspection as well as Norma's. Her short skirt swung out in a whirl of tiny pleats, her shoes and socks were gleaming and dazzlingly white, and the hat she carried in her hand that also held her racquet completed her outfit.

She had to admit to herself that she found it pleasing enough. And quite obviously Norma found it pleasing, too.

'We've talked of glamour on other occasions, my dear,' she remarked. 'Well, today you've more than your fair share of it. Remember that and it will give you courage!'

She gave Deirdre a friendly push towards the door as an impatient shout came from the other side of it.

'Coming!' Norma called, adding: 'It would have to be Charles waiting for us. He can't get to the courts quick enough.'

Deirdre picked up Blair's cardigan in her free hand and turned to follow her companion downstairs. But at the top of the stairs Norma stood aside.

'After you, Deirdre,' she said. 'This is your day. Make your entrance proudly!'

Deirdre stopped abruptly, although half-way down the stairs . . . not because of the wolf-whistle of admiration that came from Charles, but because of the older, taller figure that was standing silhouetted in the blaze of sunlight pouring through the open door behind him. He had turned quickly at the long-drawn-out whistle, and looked from Charles to the small, white, motionless form on the stairs. The expression in his eyes as he looked directly up at her, and was plainly caught completely off his guard for a moment, was nevertheless unreadable. Whether or not he admired her or even appreciated the slender grace of the picture she made Deirdre herself was unable to tell. She only knew that she wished ardently that being caught off his guard, he would give himself away.

But he did nothing of the kind. She was aware of acute disappointment, and went on descending the stairs very slowly, displaying none of the pride in the moment Norma had advised her to display.

Charles walked up to her and, taking her arm, led her down the remainder of the stairs. The admiration in his voice and look brought a tinge of appreciative colour to her cheeks, but her sense of disappointment refused to desert her.

'He's looking at me as he did that day at the railway station when I arrived,' she thought resentfully. 'We've progressed no further than that.'

The afternoon resolved itself into the familiar pattern of countless week-ends that Deirdre had known all her adult life, and the familiarity of the whole thing gradually took over and prevented her from thinking about anything else. The ping of balls came ceaselessly, white-clad figures made lightning movements in the sunshine, voices called clearly and a little dreamily in the sun-flushed atmosphere, and over all the sky was brazenly blue and utterly without sign of cloud.

Charles walked towards them and met them at the high netting fence after their first set. He spoke to Blair, his air doleful. 'We only managed to get one game. Lexia has a devil in her. She smashed at everything that was within her reach.'

Blair looked impatient, and a little grim at the same time.

'Well, it doesn't matter. We evened things up for you with our six to one.' He smiled lopsidedly, but was obviously trying to be encouraging. 'I'll tell you what, Charles,' he said. 'If you'll cheer up and get that expression of gloom off your face I'll wager you a lottery ticket that we'll go home full of champagne and victory!'

Listening to his voice, Deirdre wondered. She wondered whether it was just raillery, or whether he honestly believed they had a chance, and, if they had a chance, just how important to him it was that they should win. There was something underlying his words, something that baffled her, something provoking; something she could not place. She knew that, win or lose, no mere tennis game could achieve that difference she could sense in him.

She sat through the next couple of sets and watched from the pavilion, astonished that Blair remained by her side. He sat silent, certainly, smoking continually; but he was there. Then he was standing, handing her her racquet for the second time that day, and the unreal quality of the day itself faded, and she was back in her own familiar world of tennis.

Afternoon tea was waiting when they came off

the court. She answered questions about Cairns, laughed at the acidulous comments on her playing, and watched as Blair collected two cups of tea. 'What would you like to eat, Deirdre?' he called across to her, laughing directly for the first time that day, into her eyes. 'Will you have what I scrounge, or would you like to choose for yourself?'

Taking her silence for permission, he turned his attention to the laden tables, but Deirdre could not concentrate on the conversation going on about her. She stood, under the impact of that boldly deliberate intimate glance, that had been aimed across the brief dividing space directly into her eyes, trying to will her breath back to normal. She ate a little of the provender he had furnished, drank her tea, and took no part in the social intercourse about her.

Blair collected cups and plates, asked if anyone would care to take on his chore of captain, and laughed at the answers he received. Turning, he held out a hand to her, remarking, 'Come along, Deirdre, you can come for the ride. If I have to work, I might as well combine business with pleasure!'

She walked sedately by his side, knowing she had no option but to do so. After seeing her seated in the car, he walked round and slid under the wheel with the expert twist she had come to know so well. Making no attempt to start the engine, he reached for a cigarette and lighted it from the dashboard lighter. Then, an eyebrow high, he turned and grinned wickedly at her.

'No arguments, Deirdre. Tell me, what caused such acquiescence?' As she remained silent, he added softly, 'I've come to the conclusion you rate some recompense after the way you have worked so hard for us this afternoon. Would you like to go on a sight-seeing tour of the district?' The other brow rose to join its fellow as he continued, 'You can't move any further away than the door, you know; so I suppose I can venture to tell you how much I enjoyed our games today.'

He let in the clutch, and as the car started forward, asked her, 'Would you care to look over the tobacco factory? I'm sure that's the kind of thing that would interest you. Now,' his voice took on the tone she remembered he had used when speaking of Mrs. Malcombe's little girl that night at Lexia's place, 'now, some girls I know would rather have the romantic setting of the river for their sight-seeing.'

Sitting silently in her corner, she was not to be drawn, and for the next half-hour she saw what Nerada had to offer. She enjoyed it in a way, then sat back wondering where they were going as the big car turned away from town, moving very fast.

It pulled in to stop on a slight eminence. Deirdre was enchanted. She could see for miles . . . hundreds of miles, she corrected herself. She hugged her arms tight around her and gazed into the distance at the long range of mountains, standing stark and purple against the late evening sky. When she left this place she knew that at least the memory of this golden afternoon of sunshine and uncertain happiness – yes, and Blair's presence too – would hold no regrets, whatever the future brought.

Lounging back on his seat, one arm thrown carelessly along the frame of the open window, Blair was silent, smoking.

She turned impulsively. 'Thank you, Blair, very much. It's been a lovely afternoon.'

'I must say,' he answered her, 'that when you do bring yourself to do something, you do it very handsomely. Thank you too, Deirdre. Tell me, how do you like living up here? Are you happy among us?'

This time she turned directly to face him. 'Yes, indeed I am. I like the work, and everyone is so good to me. When I remember how I hated the thought of coming here . . .' She broke off, her eyes swinging away from his gaze to fasten on the horizon.

'I remember that day.' Blair's hands were clasped on the wheel now, and he was looking at her, not at the view in the distance. 'I glanced up, and there you were, as supercilious an eyeful as I had ever had the misfortune to look at. I remember asking Bert Langton what he'd brought us. You looked out over the town, then back to the station with such a glance of distaste. I imagined you classed the whole place as some noxious medicine you might have to take, but certainly couldn't be made to like.'

'I did not!' The very words were indignant. 'And

you ... *you*, to talk! You know very well the way you looked at me.' Shyness was forgotten in righteous indignation. 'Besides,' she went on, 'I was nervous. You had no such excuse. I had to get this job with Mrs. Liddle. I needed it.'

He gave a muttered ejaculation. 'Haven't you any people at all, Deirdre? It's outrageous, a young girl like you on your own.'

'Only some remote cousins,' was the uncaring reply. 'But they hardly know me, and really, I don't need them. Dr. Mac was a good friend to me, and I had a job ... and tennis,' she ended with a wry grin.

Shaking his head, he took another cigarette from a packet by his side, and reached for the car lighter. Inhaling deeply, he leant forward to return it... and missed. It plummeted down directly towards Deirdre's outstretched legs; he retrieved it, incredibly swiftly, just as it touched them, and turned a grim face at her.

'Did it burn you at all?'

'No ... no, I moved in time.' She had her legs curled under her by now. 'It's quite all right, truly, Blair.'

His hand was hard on her shoulder, his face towering over her own; his eyes, not glinting with amusement now, blazed into hers. She closed them, unable utterly to meet that glittering look, felt herself drawn close, even closer, for the fraction of a moment, then the rigid clasp on her shoulders loosened, and his voice, harsh, tight, not at all normal, said explosively, 'What blasted clumsiness to do that! It could have given you a nasty burn.'

'It doesn't matter, it really didn't. Don't you think we should go now?' Her words tumbled out breathlessly. 'It's getting late.'

He considered her a moment longer, gravely, then his customary laconic smile returning, he gave answer. 'You're right, of course. Yes, I think we *had* better be going.' Switching on the engine, he let in the clutch, and the big car shot forward.

CHAPTER SEVEN

'HAVE you a light pink lipstick, Deirdre? I seem to have mislaid mine.' Norma was putting the finishing touches to her make-up, as they dressed for the dance which was always a part of this week-end. She used the borrowed long slender tube, then spoke to the reflection of her friend in the mirror. Deirdre had been unusually quiet and withdrawn during this hectic preparation for a hurried dinner, scrambles for baths, and a time limit for being ready. 'Is everything all right? You want to go to the dance, don't you?'

Smoothing her dress as she turned to collect her evening purse and scarf, Deirdre thought; I can't tell even Norma just how much I really want to go, and why. How very much I wish I could be able to look . . . not beautiful, but somehow a little special, just for tonight. So when she did answer, her words were stilted, precise. 'Yes, very much. How does my frock look?'

The older girl took it in, from the pale lemon swathed bodice, fitting tightly into the small waist, to the many tiny pleated fullnesses ending just above her knees. It was a study in yellows and golds the faint lemon at the neckline to the dull gold of the hem.

A smile was in the voice that answered. 'You look just like you did in your tennis outfit, and you were undoubtedly a success in that.' Her gaze was a little quizzical as she saw the heightened colour in the face opposite her, and she went on gently, 'You look enchanting, Deirdre. I only hope I look half as nice. Let's go and have a wonderful time!'

The music was playing when they arrived; a gay rhythm that set the tempo for the evening. Streamers and balloons swung everywhere, the brilliant colours of dresses moving continuously caught the light, giving to the assembly a carnival effect. Smiles and called greetings met them on every hand, and Deirdre felt an upsurge of warmth for this place, for her position in it. She saw Blair in the distance with Lexia and her party – a different Blair altogether from the one to whom she was accustomed. Dressed in evening clothes he looked so outstandingly handsome, so different from the familiar figure on the tennis court; the even more casual one at home . . . her thoughts came to an abrupt stop. So this was what it had come to . . . at home.

The night wore on and she could not help but smile in sympathy every time she glanced at Norma, even if she had no smile for herself. Tony stayed beside her continuously, and Deirdre wondered idly if this was because he was not in his home town; that he showed his preference for her so openly, then concluded that this could not be so. Most people in the hall would know him. She shrugged, dismissing it from her thoughts. Her expectation of dancing with Blair had after all not materialized, and with the night so far advanced she resolutely gave her attention exclusively to her partners.

In slow tempo the music began again; a figure was standing before her, a hand outstretched. She went into the arms waiting for her without a word, gazing up at him for some sign of the friendly man of this afternoon. His expression, however, was forbidding, closed; strange for the normally laughing Blair. They circled slowly, the lights dim, the notes of the saxophone rising high and clear above the rest. Deirdre recognized the tune from an old recording her mother had had. It was a revival and they were playing a new arrangement of it tonight. She felt the arm around her waist tighten as the vocalist came to the front of the bandstand and began to sing.

'Nature patterned you, and when she was done,
'You were all the sweet things rolled into one.'

They circled more slowly still, and the words were little more than a sigh as the singer finished the chorus. Picking up the refrain once more, the saxophone swelled out sweet and high, before drifting softly to an end.

Deirdre stood still, motionless, within the circle of that arm remaining iron-tight about her. Then it slid slowly away, and he was walking her back to her seat. He thanked her gravely, and nodding to Tony, she heard him say, 'Spare me a moment, Tony. I'd like a word with you.' She watched as they walked out a few yards on to the dance floor, speak for a brief moment, then part, and continued to watch the taller one as he made his way through the throng. Apparently his party was leaving. The women collecting their wraps, the men standing by to escort them. She turned as Norma touched her arm, telling her, 'We're leaving now, Deirdre!'

She showed her astonishment. She had assumed that they would stay until the end. Marge, however, did not only look her astonishment; she was loudly vocal. 'Of course we can stay until the dance finishes,' she returned hotly. 'I'm having a wonderful time!'

Tony cut in, said shortly, 'We're leaving now. I promised Blair we would leave at once.'

That silenced Marge, who was reduced to muttering, 'I suppose Mrs. Liddle told him to see that we went. It's just like her!' she pouted, sulkily mutinous, but not dreaming of disobeying.

They walked off the dance floor, Charles and Henry joining them as they went. It was a beautiful night outside – no moon, but the Southern Cross was there, glitteringly flamboyant, showing itself off among the galaxy of brilliant pinpoints of light visible in the velvet darkness overhead.

'Shall we go and have a drink?'

The café along the street was blazing with light and well patronized, but Tony answered Henry's invitation by heading them firmly in the direction of their hotel. 'Straight home, Henry,' he reiterated. 'I assured Blair that we would. Also, we all have an early morning tomorrow.'

'Too right. I forgot about that. That settles it, we'll celebrate tomorrow night before we go home.' Charles for his part gave in cheerfully.

'Thank goodness for tennis as far as Charles is concerned,' Norma murmured softly, as Charles finished his little speech. With an arm through Marge's she hurried her along, paying absolutely no attention to her protests that *she* wasn't playing tennis tomorrow.

Deirdre raised herself drowsily on one elbow, then sank down, preparing to go back to sleep, but the knocking persisted.

'Are you awake, Miss Sheldon?'

Realization came with a rush. 'Yes . . . yes, thank you,' she answered. 'I'm awake now.'

She had left a call for six-thirty, and knowing that that allowed her very little time to waste, she made haste with her dressing. With an affectionate smile she put the coverings back across the bare shoulder in the other bed, then reached for her prayer book and gloves. She left the room quietly and tiptoed round the corner to the stairs, to come abruptly there to a complete halt.

A tall man in a deep maroon dressing gown was leaning over the balcony railing smoking a cigarette, the early morning sunlight glinting on dark hair more untidy than she had ever seen it. She watched, hypnotized, the smoke curling in lazy blue spirals from the cylinder held in that slender hand, unable to make herself just say good morning and walk past him to the steps.

'So . . . I might have known! How are you getting there, Deirdre? Is someone meeting you downstairs?' Receiving only a shake of the head, his voice sharpened. 'I know it would have been too much to expect, for you to ask me to take you. Nevertheless, with a dozen cars at your disposal, there's no necessity to walk.'

She looked directly at him and spoke pleadingly, trying to appease the very real anger in his face. 'Please, Blair, it's a lovely morning, and I like to walk. You must know how little we walk in our work.' She moved towards the stairs. 'I haven't a lot of time, it's after ten to seven,' she looked again at the intimidating countenance opposite her; but seeing no sign at all of softening, she passed him to hurry below. Outside the hotel, she stood a moment to control the slight trembling in all her limbs, then, drawing a deep breath, she walked swiftly away.

As she had told Blair, it was another glorious day. There was a sparkle and freshness which came with the earliness of the hour, but the deep blue of the heavens was the same as yesterday, and a great many yesterdays before that. She went quickly, past houses encircled by emerald lawns. Tropical flowers ran riot, and their more cultivated sisters gave forth a perfume to compliment the day which God had given. Her eyes on the colour, blazing purple, lavender, crimson, pink, the gold and blue of the day; she knew thankfulness that she had been granted this period of time, even if heartache and loneliness did follow. Again she drew in a deep breath and unconsciously her pace grew faster.

Leaving church immediately the service ended, nevertheless, she was caught and hailed by one of the tournament players whom she had met yesterday. Saying 'How do you do', politely, trying to remember names, she found herself hemmed in as more of the congregation poured out of the building behind her. Knowing also that breakfast at the hotel would have already started, she kept an eye on her watch while trying to answer the invitations so lavishly being offered.

Flustered a little by this overwhelming hospitality, she did not notice a car pull into the curb. The door opened and closed and Blair was by her side. It wasn't a case of introductions. He was besieged from all directions. Apparently he could answer half a dozen questions at once, too, or so it seemed to her as he took hold of her arm.

'I'm after our young fugitive here,' he replied to the most persistent. 'We have to be on the court at nine-thirty, so I expect I'd better see that she's fed and ready. Afterwards, of course, we have to find enough courage to play your number one pair.'

'Don't think you're going to have all your own way in that set,' a laughing voice put in. 'We'll all be praying for your defeat!'

Blair cast one rueful glance at the church behind them, let his gaze drift back to the smiling faces. Finally his eyes rested on Deirdre. 'It looks then, doesn't it, as if it all depends on my partner here, in more ways than one.' He waved a hand in farewell, and, followed by laughter they stepped into the car. It shot swiftly away.

'It was no trouble, I know I needn't have met you. Shall we leave it at that, Deirdre?' He forestalled the words trembling upon her lips; his voice was curt, abrupt. The car pulled into the hotel driveway. His, 'Be out here at nine-fifteen, please,' was equally curt as he let her make her own way into the entrance.

Punctually at a quarter past nine they were waiting. Blair, with Lexia's hand through his arm, joined them. He nodded to Norma, told her, 'I'll take you, too,' and put them both in the back seat. He seated Lexia, then walked round and slid under the wheel. Extracting a cigarette from a packet in his shirt pocket, he automatically reached for the car lighter. His eyes came up abruptly to meet Deirdre's gaze in the rear vision mirror. The recollection of yesterday was there and she felt a warm colour surge into her face at the hard unsmiling challenge in those so blue eyes.

The car jumped forward, and gazing out of her window, Deirdre saw none of the sights that had so pleased her on her way to church this morning . . . only a slim brown hand reaching incredibly swiftly for a lighter before it could burn her, and a voice saying, 'Yes, I think we *had* better be going!'

Charles was again waiting for them as they walked off the court after finishing their set. He appealed to Blair, 'Come and watch us for a while, Blair. With you there Lexia might show that she can play tennis – and she really can when she wants to.'

For a moment, observing the frown on his face, Deirdre expected him to give an unequivocal refusal, then his normally good-humoured grin made its appearance. He spoke, almost inaudibly, to Charles, who flushed but smiled with relief, then went on in his more normal tone, 'The trouble with you, Charles, my lad, is that everything has to be subordinated to this damned tennis. You'd better watch out – as the song says – or it'll be running you. Oh well, just a minute.' He crossed to the pavilion to leave his racquet and collect his sweater, also catching up the one he had diverted for the season to Deirdre's use at the same time. He came behind her, dropping it over her shoulders on the way past. With a casual, 'I'll see you later,' he departed with Charles.

Deirdre went across to the far court to wait for Norma. 'Will you walk back to the hotel with me?' she asked her friend when she came off. 'I want to collect those chocolates I ordered for Mrs. Liddle.'

'O.K., Deirdre But we'd first better tell someone that we're leaving.'

They strolled slowly along the verge of the long gravel road leading into town, both silent, absorbed in their own thoughts. It was hot, Deirdre acknowledged, but it was not an enervating heat. Her glance went back towards the courts, and she drew a sigh of contentment. Such a scene was the same everywhere tennis was played; be it Wimbledon or a small country town such as this was.

She spoke across to Norma then, dreams in her voice. 'It's been a week-end to remember, Norma, hasn't it?'

The older girl laughed, and her words were brisk, rallying, 'You won't think so, going home with Charles, if we don't catch up a few more games!'

Deirdre laughed too. 'Oh, it's only a pose with him. He would like to win . . . so would we all, but I'm sure he doesn't really care. Why, he can belt a ball back and forth for hours, without playing a proper game the whole afternoon. Did you enjoy the dance last night?' she went on in an altogether different tone.

Norma's smile was reminiscent, then she sighed. 'Yes, I did, Deirdre. I wish . . .' she stopped, was

124

silent a moment. 'I do wish it was all straightforward between Tony and me. I don't talk about it, but I fell in love with him when we first met.' She grinned then, remembering. 'I must have had a nerve, I'm sure he didn't even notice me. I was seventeen and gawky, and he was a star, completely beyond reach. He was kind, handsome – oh, not as handsome as Blair, of course,' (Oh, of course, Deirdre reflected caustically) 'and nice, Deirdre, so nice.' (Which Blair is definitely not, Deirdre also reflected caustically.) There was silence for a while as they plodded along.

'But why, Norma?' Deirdre could keep quiet no longer. 'Why . . . ? It seems so stupid to me. You're both young and healthy. You have the same interests; and there's no family feud separating two star-crossed lovers in the Shakespearean tradition. And,' she continued vehemently, 'anyone with half an eye can see you're made for each other.'

Norma smiled ruefully at the younger girl's fervency. 'I know, Deirdre. As you say . . .' But she sighed again. 'Tony doesn't say very much, you know; but occasionally something slips through. It leads me to think that there could be other arrangements expected of him. And of course, there's religion – or should I say, the difference in it. However, I've waited for so long, I can wait a little longer. I've noticed too that Tony's attitude has changed just lately. It seems much more possessive. And he seeks out my company – so much so, in fact, compared to previously, that I have to remind myself not to expect too much, in case. . . . Well, we'll see.'

They collected their chocolates from a café doing a roaring business, then strolled leisurely back to the hotel. 'Do you propose to shock Marge again, Deirdre, by showering and changing into yet another set of whites?' Norma asked as Deirdre flopped on to the bed. Marge had been loudly vocal about the amount of tennis clothes Deirdre had packed for, as she called it, one lousy little week-end. She was answered drowsily from a face buried deep in a pillow. 'Not now, after lunch.' Deirdre was hearing a saxophone's notes rising high and clear, feeling a man's arm holding her, growing even tighter as they swelled, then faded to a whisper. She wasn't interested in showers . . . or tennis, as she held close the recollection, to keep for remembrance, when she was gone from here.

Eating her lunch slowly, without a glance at the table in the far corner, a touch on the shoulder brought her head round. Her face broke into the warm smile she always accorded Bill Darrell.

'I only wanted to wish you luck for this afternoon, Deirdre,' he said. 'Keep the flag of Lim flying high, won't you?'

'I'll try, Bill,' she smiled her thanks, her gaze going beyond to where Blair, his eyes narrowed and sardonic, waited with the two women.

All interest centred on the game in progress; no one spared a glance for Blair as he arrived and dropped into a seat at Deirdre's side to await their turn to play Nerada's number one pair. Suddenly she felt the form, so close beside her, begin to shake uncontrollably, and she looked round quickly, wondering.

He gave her what Tony called his wicked grin, still shaking silently with laughter. He answered her gaze, murmuring softly, 'I was merely wondering what would be the reaction if we got beaten six-love.'

She turned shocked eyes to him. 'Oh no, Blair, we won't,' she protested anxiously. 'We won't, will we?'

His grin was still in evidence. This time he was grinning at her. 'I don't expect we will, with you playing, my little one, but I couldn't help wondering if we would really be outcasts if such a thing were to happen.'

She followed his glance around the intent faces, Charles's especially. Her own mouth began to tremble; however, she quickly suppressed her laughter as she met that look of his, challenging, mischief-bent, and turned from him as a burst of clapping heralded the end of the set.

'Well, that six-three win leaves us two down.' Blair's voice now was level, matter-of-fact. 'Here we go!' He reached down a hand for her, and she walked with him out into the sunlight.

Discussing the match afterwards, when asked to recall a certain point, Deirdre would just shrug. She had concentrated so desperately on trying to return every ball; that was her aim, her only interest. At three-all, each player had retained their own service, and Blair serving in his turn kept his. Crossing over, he leant over to her and murmured, 'Well, at least we've given them a run for their money!'

She merely nodded, not wanting to talk. Then, with the score against their opponents, Mrs. Reaston had served a double fault. A groan had come from everyone in sympathy. From then onwards, Deirdre remembered only serving, serving, serving, thinking desperately that no one would ever get the deciding points; but abruptly Blair's arm was flung across her shoulders, he was guiding her to the net to shake hands. He had also laughed down at her as they walked off, saying, 'There you are, Deirdre! Charles will be your slave for life now. Would you care to be chatelaine of the Wilson farm?' He had time to say no more; they were surrounded, and sure enough, Charles did not only put his arm around her as he had done once before. He hugged her tight and danced up and down. And across his shoulder, blue glinting eyes had looked back into hers and shown only satisfaction.

She had been very glad to sink back into the corner of Henry's car, when at long last it was time to start for home. Blair and Bert Langton patrolled the long convoy, to check that none of the jubilant celebrants were missing; and she watched them, curled up with the big cardigan around her, content.

With his arm around Yvonne, Bill also lounged in his corner, allowing Henry to send the car hurtling swiftly into the night; and looking out at the flying countryside, Deirdre sat back and hugged the memory of the whole week-end to her.

Emerging from the car which stopped with the usual spurt of gravel right before their quarters. Deirdre and Marge just stood, too tired to make an effort. Mrs. Liddle's voice, however, soon made an end to that. Coming towards them from the direction of Charles's car, she was saying in no uncertain tones: 'And have you talking tennis till midnight? – no, thank you!' Her trenchant refusal of his offer to carry over the cases made even Deirdre smile a little in spite of the deadly tiredness possessing her. They heard her continue, 'We have your father's tobacco to finish this week, in case you don't know.' And Charles, who was never sulky, came very close to it as he muttered, 'I do know. It's my tobacco too, you know.'

The reply he received was only a 'humph' from half-way between the house and the quarters.

The two girls said their thank-yous to Henry as he dropped their cases inside the doorway, and heard him speak to Mrs. Liddle and Norma on his way back to the car. With a roar it started up, the gravel spurting from under the wheels as he took off.

Marge gave a tired imitation of her wide grin. 'If only his parents could hear their car now,' she said, 'I bet he would be driving the farm utility for a long time to come. He must be doing sixty. On a dirt road too.' She yawned widely. 'Work tomorrow!' With an eye on their mentor, she suggested innocently, 'I don't suppose we could take tomorrow morning off to sleep, and make it up some other time?'

'You suppose right, my girl, and if you don't get off to bed quick smart, and be ready to begin work in the morning, there'll be some other supposing to do!'

Marge sighed, said resignedly. 'Well, there was no harm in trying it on, was there?'

Deirdre grinned in sympathy and followed her to her own cubicle. She slid back the catches of her case and shrugged at the pile of soiled white clothes that met her sight, wondering when she could possibly find time to launder them; thinking that they would probably have to wait till next week-end. A tender smile curled her lips. Any amount of extra work was well worth the two days just spent. They would remain for ever written on her heart.

Taking up Mrs. Liddle's chocolates, she walked down to the end cubicle and placed them on her table. She put her head round Edna's curtains, but the bed was empty. Still, she hadn't Mrs. Liddle to tell her what to do. Deirdre giggled a little as she returned to her own small space. She, who had been running her own life since she was sixteen, now did exactly as she was told by that caustic, abrupt, but wonderfully kind individual who ruled their working lives.

CHAPTER EIGHT

TOBACCO. ... It seemed mountain-high to Deirdre in the next few days, knowing that it needed consistent effort on all their parts to see it finished by the week-end. In the grip of a lethargy she was unable to shake off, her laundry remained still in its laundry bag, and she lay evening after evening in the long chair, listless, unmoving. A thought grew in her mind, frightening, but Mrs. Liddle soon made short work of that. 'Ill? Don't be more foolish than you have to be, Deirdre. Naturally you're tired. You've been putting all your spare time into practice, evening after evening, and although that in itself wouldn't make you as languid as you are, I expect that knowing how much everyone wanted to win for this once, and how important your contribution to that end was, your nervous system is now taking its toll. It's over now, and this is the inevitable let down. Rest a few days, certainly. Then you'll see. You'll be your own self by the week-end.' Astringent, incisive, Deirdre could feel a reluctant grin at herself already on her lips.

Then, almost at once it seemed, Friday was upon them. The last rows of ungraded tobacco were dwindling and they knew that today indeed would see the finish of it. But it was as they were having their morning tea that the first intimation of what was in store for them made its appearance. The farm truck drove up and David with two of his young friends jumped out of a back piled high with greenery. Paying no attention to the tea-drinkers outside, they made their way into the interior of the shed. Charles stepped from the utility's cabin, and strolled across, a wide grin on his face.

'We weren't going to tell you,' he exclaimed, 'but Mum says as the boys are going to decorate the place, you'd better know. We're putting on a party tonight, to celebrate the end of the grading. A real humdinger, square-dancing party,' he continued. 'Also, it's to be in the nature of a victory party for last week-end.'

'Really, Charles,' came from Norma, 'how in the world are you going to set about decorating now? We have tobacco all over the place, and it'll be too late to begin by the time we've finished.'

Charles wasn't in the least disconcerted. His answer was casual, knowing. 'Wait and see. In fact, come along and start seeing now.'

Curiously they followed him through the big doorway. The three boys were carting huge armfuls of the stacked tobacco across to the grading benches, then, having completely emptied one end of the big room, they got to work with brushes and brooms, and soon it was spotlessly bare.

Deirdre was fascinated. She was trying to grade and watch too. Never in her life had she seen anything so ruthless, yet so methodical. They knew what they were doing, these boys, and went straight without deviation to their goal, and heaven help what got in their way. They must have done this before, she reflected, watching them at work with a ball of twine, hammer, and tacks. Admiringly she stood still, gazing at the far window. It was a work of art. A voice said dryly in her ear, 'We shall be working still when the dance begins if you don't get a move on, Deirdre.'

She started guiltily, said at once, 'Yes, I know, but aren't they amazing?'

By afternoon tea-time, the boys were abreast of the grading benches, and Deirdre, only half jesting, remarked that if they didn't quickly finish what tobacco remained, she could see it, and themselves as well, being ruthlessly swept right out of the door.

They each drank a cup standing when the tea came over, and received wide-toothed understanding grins from the three demons as these latter heaved the residue of their task up on to the benches for them, and by five o'clock it was actually finished; the last leaf graded and stacked away.

Mrs. Liddle gave a huge sigh, smiled her rare smile at all impartially, said, 'Well, that's that. Finished on time.' There was deep satisfaction in her voice.

Edna stretched, contentment oozing from the tips of her toes to her outflung arms. 'I'm for a bath, a long, long bath, and I want no banging on the door till I'm through,' she said. She went out, and the others followed, slowly, lazily.

Trailing behind, on a sudden impulse, Deirdre walked across to a bulkshed beside the towering curing barns. She stood in the doorway, her glance roving it, satisfaction at a job completed flooding her. Charles's father was busy bulking some of the just finished leaf; but crowding the larger half of the shed were square, compact, hessian-covered bales – a great many of them. She remembered how fascinated she had been the very first time she had watched these bales being formed, at her first farm; at Brandt's – a million years ago, it now seemed. Watched the big mangle-like contraption manipulate and press, and when both man and machine appeared satisfied, eject them, regulation size, and ready, to await the all-important happening of the year: the sales.

She remembered also, as she stood there, Norma's unfailing patience, as she had shown and re-shown Deirdre how to tie, using a smaller leaf of the same grade. Deirdre would watch the neatly folded strip of tobacco twirled swiftly around a handful of leaf, then with an expert flick of the wrist it was securely fastened, not a stem protruding from its trimly bandaged top. She recalled her own unhandy attempts, and the conviction that she would never accomplish such an intricate manoeuvre. If for nothing else – and there was – she would always think of Norma with affection, for her matter-of-fact attitude at that time. She never flapped, she never got short-tempered with Deirdre's clumsiness. She only explained and demonstrated. Then suddenly, unexpectedly, Deirdre had found herself with a hand of tobacco, done automatically, unconsciously, as she spoke to Edna, which was as neatly tied, and as expertly, as any in the shed.

She gave a last look round the now darkening building, left, and sauntered past the outbuildings on her way to the quarters. She saw Edna come from the shower annex, and wondered with slight interest whether she was seriously interested in Stan Bolton. They had certainly been a constant twosome. Edna had not even accompanied them to Nerada for the tennis finals, pleading a previous engagement with Stan.

Thinking of her, Deirdre realized that while Edna was attractive, apt to draw all eyes, she was also extremely practical. She might weigh Stan's good points against his bad, the general hurly-burly of living when there was not as much money as there might have been. Stan was a wonderful dancer, and on the dance floor, together, they were a wonderful pair. There was only one man who danced better than Stan, and that was Blair.

Suddenly, overwhelmingly, Deirdre's need of Blair blotted out all other thoughts. She could feel his arms around her, as if he was actually holding her . . . feel his lips caressing, demanding, and drawing the very heart out of her. She shut her eyes tightly, leaning against the corner post, utter desolation welling over her because she had, she knew, to make up her mind once and for all that her life had to be lived without Blair and his caresses, and she must get used to the bitterness of this knowledge.

The tang of eucalyptus, pungent, aromatic, was one of the impressions that greeted the girls when they arrived at the shed later. Not a sign of the old familiar place was to be seen. It was a fairyland, a bower of greenery. Streamers and balloons, hundreds of them, were suspended from the ceiling, and Deirdre smiled inwardly, thinking of Charles purloining anything at the house he could lay his hands on to enable him to create this scene of colour and enchantment.

An elderly man seated in a corner had an accordion slung carelessly across his knee. No small accordion this; it was a whopper. A younger edition of him stood nearby holding a fiddle. Gay and colourful blouses and skirts caught the light, scintilating as they merged and parted. They were a uniform for young and old. Some were really beautiful, others home-made cottons. But all had one thing in common. They had plenty of material in each and every one, and they were all bright and eye-catching.

She had never square-danced, and had no idea at all how to go about it. When told, Charles replied that that condition would be remedied before the night was over.

And, sinking down breathlessly at the end of the pre-supper dance, she realized he had been proved right. She certainly knew now how to square-dance. But breathless was the operative word. She wondered whether she would ever breathe evenly again, and also whether her feet would ever be just again something on the end of her legs, and not the aching appendages they now were. She said to Henry, and meant it, that she could work for a week and not use up half the energy she used in just one square dance.

He grinned, and answered in his slow drawl, 'But work isn't half as pleasant, is it, Deirdre?' and, laughing ruefully, she had to admit that it was not.

Only this she did know. Unlike other dances, it left no time to wonder why one particular person was not present, or to be able to think much about it, if he wasn't. The only impression allowed was a kaleidoscope of flying colourful movement, compulsive music, rhythmical clapping, and the stamping of many feet. This was a new way of dancing and allowed no outside influence to penetrate its preserve.

Glancing the length of the brightly lighted room, at the laughing crowd so obviously enjoying itself, she thought of the care and preparation a party such as this must have entailed, and knew a sadness that she would be gone from here tomorrow with no thought of returning.

Eating her supper slowly, silent, scarcely listening to the hum of conversation around her, she suddenly learned the reason for Blair's absence. Lounging against one of David's decorated windows, a group of older men were discussing tobacco . . . a very normal procedure up here on any occasion, dance or no. He was in Nerada on tobacco business. With this exception, all the tennis crowd was present, even to Lexia, who, Deirdre had to admit, looked ravishing. Her skirt was definitely not home-made. It was the colour of the sea, the colour one saw in the shallows off Green Island at home. Green, translucent, it shimmered as she moved. Combined with an off-the-shoulder, very low cut, sheer white blouse, it was an outfit to make a plain girl beautiful. It made of Lexia a picture to enrapture any eye, Deirdre reflected hopelessly.

Gathering up her supper dishes, she slipped outside and found Mrs. Wilson, who was still very much occupied with food at one of the long white-draped benches. 'Let me help, Mrs. Wilson,' Deirdre pleaded. 'There's so much clearing up to be done.'

But she was firmly rejected with a decisive, 'Not tonight, Deirdre. This is your party. Run along like a good girl. There's the music starting up again.'

'No, truly, Mrs. Wilson, I simply couldn't dance another step. I couldn't.' Deirdre held her ground. 'This square-dancing is like top-grade tennis. You have to get into training for it. Now, you take

Marge. She might have thought I was good at tennis – well, I think she's more than good at that Indian fire stomp they're getting ready for in there. I don't believe even Mrs. Liddle could get her away before God Save the Queen tonight.

'It's been a wonderful party, Mrs. Wilson,' she went on, her gaze roving across this familiar place. 'I'll always remember tonight. Thank you for giving it.'

'Yes, it has turned out well, hasn't it?' Deirdre felt her lips twitch at the complacency so apparent in the older woman's tone, but lost her smile at the next words. 'I hope there'll be a lot more of them, Deirdre, and that next year your feet will allow you to dance all night. You know,' her hostess busied herself among the crockery, 'we've been very happy to have you here with us, and hope you'll come again next season.'

It was Deirdre's turn now to be busy amongst the cups and saucers. She spoke slowly, haltingly. 'We'll have to wait and see, dear Mrs. Wilson. I simply don't know what I'm doing after I finish up here.' She felt embarrassed, a traitor; knowing perfectly well that the one thing she would not be doing would be to return here.

Later she stood in the doorway, watching what Mr. Wilson had announced as the last dance, taking in again, fascinated, the intricate steps, the flash of colour, the rhythm of the irresistible music. Then, abruptly, it was over. The players went into 'The

Queen' and everyone was singing. Dierdre felt tears sting her eyelids and blinked quickly to dispel them, telling herself not to be silly. Of course it sounded well. Men's voices in bulk always did, and at tonight's party they had predominated.

Mothers were bundling children, warm and snug, carefully into back seats of cars. One after another they took off, and Deirdre heard as the last of them stopped at the fence to close the gate, 'Good night, Good night, coo . . . ee . . . eeee!'

Mr. Wilson broke in on her reverie, no nostalgia-after-the-party feeling in his voice. It was jovial and deeply satisfied. 'Anyone care for a last cup of tea?' He had one of the smaller tea-pots in his hand, from the spout of which issued curling white vapour.

'No, really, Mr. Wilson. You couldn't possibly eat another thing, could you? After all that supper!' Deirdre was incredulous.

'Who said anything about eating, Deirdre? Drinking tea isn't eating.' There was a twinkle in his eye as he looked at her.

'I'll have a cup, Charlie.' Mrs. Liddle held out a cup to be filled. 'But these girls had better get off to bed,' she added. 'It's been a long week, and we want to get over to Blair's early tomorrow. I need to talk to you, anyway.'

He gave a mock groan. 'Talking to me means money! After the cheque I wrote out today, I shall have to watch out I don't starve before my next crop.'

'I doubt it,' was the dry retort. 'Only imagine, if we make a lot of money grading the leaf, how much more you must make, selling it.'

The girls gave him looks of commiseration, knowing who would win in any battle of words, then drifted off. They were all tired and a new order began tomorrow.

CHAPTER NINE

EVERY mile the truck travelled closer to the Cameron farms Deirdre became more nervous. She sat between Mrs. Liddle and Marge inside the cabin, when normally she would have preferred to sit in the back with Norma and Edna. But early this morning she had barred the inside. She felt that to be beside Mrs. Liddle gave her some small feeling of security.

Beside her, on her face a rapt expression that told of memories of last night, Marge stirred suddenly. 'We should be smelling the oleanders any time now,' she observed.

Deirdre looked her surprise. It seemed a strange remark to make, out here running along a bush road.

'Are there trees around here?' she wanted to know.

Marge stared at her. 'Haven't you heard about the oleanders, Deirdre?' The girl sitting by her side smiled, Mrs. Liddle smiled too; or rather she put on her vulture grin, which was what Deirdre called it in the privacy of her own mind.

She said now, 'You'll soon be driving through an avenue of them, Deirdre.'

'And you'll soon be smelling them, too,' Marge ejaculated.

'Blair's mother,' the older woman went on, 'loved oleanders. She only lived a few years after they came to this farm, but she planted them all around the house – that is, the old house, the one we'll be quartered in for the duration of our stay.'

'I've never heard of an avenue of oleanders before,' Deirdre said slowly, thinking about it.

Mrs. Liddle chuckled. 'It was actually a gesture on Blair's part,' she told Deirdre. 'Some seasonal workers were up here looking for work and, inquiring at the pub, were referred to Blair, as he was known to need extra hands. "Oh, but we've tried there," they'd answered. "That's the place of the oleanders, isn't it? The big boss from there is away out of town".'

'And often afterwards,' she went on, 'Blair was still greeted with, "And how's the place of the oleanders, oh, big boss?" When he moved out of the old place and built his new home closer to the boundary of the property, he planted this broad avenue of flowers. It's exactly what he would do, like throwing down the gage in olden times.' Mrs. Liddle mused for a moment, then as if continuing a line of thought, said slowly, 'It might have been a gage, but they must entail a great deal of work.'

'And they're never scraggy either, are they, Mrs. Liddle?' Marge interjected. 'Oleanders do tend to look uncared for, unless a lot of attention is paid to them. But I love to come here every year for the first time, and be sort of greeted by their perfume as we come close to the farm.'

Arriving at a barred gate, and even feeling the way she did, Deirdre still had to smile as Edna jumped down to open it. Norma, apparently, was running true to form. Driving the truck through, Mrs. Liddle gazed about her as she waited for Edna to climb back.

'I always feel sad when I come out here to Blair's farm,' she murmured. 'It brings back the old days when his parents were alive and he was only a baby. Well,' she gave a final glance round before letting in the clutch, 'things have certainly changed since that time.'

From her seat in the middle, Deirdre sat thinking of that last remark. She couldn't visualize Blair as a baby, not even as a boy; only as a confident, arrogant, sure of himself man. For a fleeting moment she wondered how other people saw him.

Not all of the trees in the long straight avenue were in bloom, but the deep glowing pink blossoms flaunted their colour and perfume in sufficient profusion to make of the driveway a delight. To Deirdre, who had known oleanders all her life, this vividly green, carefully tended volume of trees took on an elegance hitherto not associated with the more common variety she was used to in almost every garden at home.

She forgot both, the trees and the fragrance, as the truck came to the end of the avenue and drove slowly past the house nestling in its framework of flowering trees and shrubs. Not that one could see a great deal of it, but the glimpse which she caught of rose red brick, delicately wrought iron, and the glitter of glass, through trellises covered with honeysuckle, with the royal purple of bougainvillea, triumphant over all, added yet another facet to the complex character that she knew without the faintest shadow of doubt was the lodestone of her existence. Then they were past, and past too, the emerald green lawns surrounding the house, on which, even at this early hour, sprinklers were sending their jets of water high into the air.

After leaving behind what seemed to her endless rows of drying barns and bulk sheds, they pulled up before a house similar to the Wilson place, only smaller. Norma handed down the suitcases and parcels from the back, and, collecting her own paraphernalia, Deirdre followed Mrs. Liddle, thinking, this is it, I'm actually on Blair's farm!

'Isn't it nice? I love to come here and have a house all to ourselves.' Marge was dancing about, her dress swirling around her as she pivoted the length of the room. Deirdre followed the still dancing form as it moved through the doorway to the back of the house and stopped by the table in the kitchen's centre. Against one side stood a wooden stove, but one of the more modern kind. Shelves and cupboards lining the walls gleamed. Their pristine freshness suggesting either careful housekeeping or a recent application of paint. Curtains fluttered suddenly, sunbeams catching at their gay colours as Marge threw open windows, then Mrs. Liddle was there beside them speaking to Norma as she walked further into the room.

'I'm getting across to see Blair, Norma. You girls had better settle in. There are only two bedrooms, share them between you. I'll sleep on the verandah and dress in the bathroom.' She raised a dismissive hand at their protests, saying definitely: 'I would prefer it that way. We take it in turns to prepare meals – Norma can put you in the picture,' this latter with an encompassing glance at the two new additions to her family, 'and I expect you'll get accustomed to it as we go along.' Ever sparing of words, that was all the explanation she ventured, as she turned to go across to the big house.

A refrigerator standing in one corner caught Deirdre's attention and she walked over to open it. 'Did I imagine that we stopped in town to buy meat and such at the shops?' she inquired of the room in general.

Edna came to stand beside her. 'Well,' there was satisfaction in her voice, 'I'm hungry already.'

Deirdre swung round. 'Does this stuff belong to us, Norma?'

'Are there chickens there, among other things?' Norma was calm, her voice matter-of-fact. 'Blair always sends two over every week-end we're here. There's a big wire-netting enclosure full of them, fowls, I mean, on the river bank further down from us. They don't cost Blair anything – apart from the looking after – as the grain for them is grown here on the farm.'

'Besides the poultry,' Deirdre was taking stock, 'there are two large bottles of milk, and yes, a big jar of cream; also a great bowl full of eggs!' She closed the fridge door and made her way to the cupboards.

'You won't find anything in those,' Norma interjected. She was grinning. 'As you know, Deirdre, our board was taken out of the money we earned at the other farms. Here, as Blair doesn't board us, we get the cheques clear. He doesn't take money for the rent of this house – which he claims goes with the grading – and Mrs. Liddle wouldn't allow him to provide so much as a grain of salt if she had her way. However, she can't refuse home-grown farm produce which he grows for himself and has plenty of. Do you know,' she added reminiscently, 'I'll swear he goes out of his way to provide them, too, because he knews how she hates to be beholden to anyone; but with it all he accords to her a deference I've certainly not seen him give to anyone else.'

No, Deirdre reflected, remembering him in all his moods, that was one state of mind she could never accuse him of. Deference indeed!

Norma was walking towards the back door. 'Come and see what I expect is out here,' she said. It swung backwards into a cemented laundry. On a bench was stacked a pyramid of paw-paws ranging from ripe golden yellow to the immaturity of dark green. Grenadillas in careful rows; a huge dish of purple passion fruit, and, pendent from the ceiling, were two bunches of bananas, these also showing the colours of gold and green.

'There should be no difficulty about dessert for dinner, anyway,' Edna commented, after they had taken it all in. 'Plenty of fruit and plenty of cream.'

'Oh, gosh,' Norma began guiltily, 'I'd better get the fire going if we're to have roast chicken for lunch, or Mrs. Liddle will have something to say.'

Deirdre's eyes had taken in the laundry. 'Do you need any help, Norma,' she inquired. 'If not, I'd like to make a start on my washing.'

'No. Get on with your laundry by all means, Deirdre. I know how much you have to do. Do you know how to light a wood copper?' A casual glance at Deirdre's rueful face caused her to say lightly, 'Not to worry, I'll hurry with the stove, then show you.'

Deirdre walked back upstairs and out to the verandah to collect her laundry bag. She stood for a few brief moments, not looking towards the house along the lane, but breathing deeply of the oleander-scented air, then swinging her burden before her she retraced her footsteps.

The fire was already glowing brightly in the stove, she noticed as she passed, and Norma was kneeling in front of the open iron door of the copper. She watched, fascinated, as the older girl put first paper, then tiny chips, then larger billets of wood into its gaping interior. It seemed to her a miracle that, in seconds, the fire was roaring up under the bright, burnished copper bowl.

Soap bubbles on the plates gleamed iridescent as she passed them from the washing-up dish into the clean rinsing water standing beside it. For the moment Deirdre felt wrapped in a cocoon of passive acceptance. Her ironing was finished, her drip-drys hung away; the dinner she had cooked for the first time today – which while maybe not as good as Norma's effort of yesterday was well appreciated. She now had the intention of going to bed for the rest of the Sunday afternoon with a new novel.

She returned Mrs. Liddle's question of wouldn't she change her mind and come with them with a negative nod, adding, 'I'm just too tired. Today I want nothing more than to be lazy. That incessant tennis; the tournament, also,' she grinned at the dour face opposite her, 'we weren't loafing that last week at the Wilson place. And,' she added emphatically, 'that dashed square-dancing was certainly no help in the retaining of energy! No,' she reiterated, 'give my love to the Brandts, and have a swim for me in the little creek. It's different, isn't it, from that one out there,' nodding to where the river ran, only a few yards away from them. Here the

150

bank was very high, the ground sloping down steeply from an escarpment; the water running deep and swift a long way below.

Wiping her soapy hands, she followed the older woman to wave good-bye, then turned without a glance in the direction of the big house, and closed the front door gently. She knew that it was empty, that Blair was in Cairns, but it had the same effect on her as its arrogant owner and she resolutely kept her eyes averted from it. Today there was no sign of life at all, no sprinklers arching their water jets far and wide on the lawns. She turned with a tiny sigh and determinedly attacked the washing-up.

Working at Blair's was the same as working at the other farms she had been at, reflected Deirdre disconsolately, except that she had seen much more of him at those same other farms than she did on his own. She had thought about and expected so much from this move, but after seeing nothing at all of him but a figure perched on a tractor in a faraway paddock, or around the fences where the silver wire glittered endlessly as it joined the posts together in a never-ending parade, she had taken herself severely to task, and turned her thoughts harshly away from him whenever they strayed in that direction.

The days passed, hardly noticed, working, swimming in the evenings, pictures or dances on Saturday nights, tennis or swimming at the week-end. Twice Blair had given parties. Stan had escorted Mrs.

Liddle and Edna across and the girls at home had heard music and laughter. The other two had treated it as a matter of course, normal procedure, and had not even discussed it. Then, out of the blue, one evening after work as she was slipping into a swim-suit, an idle remark of Marge's brought Deirdre up short. She continued with her dressing, but thought incredulously, It can't be. Only another ten days here! Just the rest of this little week, and only one whole one, left!

She sat out on the bank while the others swam, admitting it was true, but unable to credit that their two months here would be up so soon. At the beginning, a couple of months had seemed a lifetime, not to be looked beyond. Now, when finished here, only two small farms remained, and her season with Mrs. Liddle was over. There was other grading, she knew, but she knew also that when she finished with Mrs. Liddle she had finished up here.

Marge called to her, and she rose slowly, realizing that she had better make a start if she was to swim at all that evening. She dived cleanly, and struck out strongly, thinking that at least this was one of the things she had learnt to do well up here. At home, on the beaches, one would swim a few yards, let the waves knock one over, then swim another few yards and play about. At least that was what she and most other girls did. With the men, it was of course entirely different. They could really swim. But up here, in this running fresh water, there was no place to stand. It wasn't like Brandts' little creek. It was deep.

Her mood of dejection was with her still, when they went up to change for dinner. After it was over, and unable to settle to anything, she walked outside to lean against the verandah railing. The fragrance of the oleanders was strong tonight. She decided that she had not really noticed their perfume for some time; perhaps the overriding odour of tobacco which they were among all day produced that effect. On an impulse she walked down the steps and along the little bush path which ran along the top of the river bank. She turned into an ill-defined track leading down the steep slope through a break in the trees. Carpeted with tangled underbrush on both sides, nevertheless it was her favourite spot on the farm; a small, easily accessible, grassy plateau. It was a peaceful location with a serenity she found soothing. She had often come here of a morning while waiting for work to begin.

Tonight, though, there were no voices of Mrs. Turley or of the children sounding across the river, only rectangles of light discernible in the darkness. No brilliant white moon either, as there had been the last time she had sat outside, on the night of the Wilsons' impromptu party. Suddenly a dog barked across the river, a door opened, and a burst of music came echoing over the water.

She sat, chin in hand, dreaming. A rustle in the undergrowth brought her round quickly, then she was scrambling to her feet. She stumbled on the steep path, and two hands, firm and impersonal, took hold of her shoulders and drew her gently backwards.

'You shouldn't be sitting here at night, Deirdre, you know,' the so familiar voice said quietly. 'You may not have seen any, but there are snakes here, especially on the river bank among all this grass. It might be permissible to sit here in the daytime, but never at night.'

Unable to move, she stood there, his hands holding her firmly, her whole body feeling the hard, tensile length of him against her, hardly taking in what he was saying; saying – even for him – so very softly, his breath stirring the tendrils on top of her head as he spoke.

'How ... how ... did you know I was here?' Her answer when it did come was breathless, stammering.

'You forget, Deirdre, this is my place. Whatever happens on it I know about. I know, for instance—' the very low voice above her lost its gravity. It had the old customary ring of laughter, 'I know, for instance,' he repeated, 'that this particular part of the farm is one of your favourite locations, which of course is none of my business. ...' Abruptly he stopped as if thinking of something, 'However,' he resumed, 'it's very definitely my business when you come and take chances at night. I've been waiting for you to return, and as you didn't, I thought I'd better come along and find out just how irresponsible you were being. Which was as well. You couldn't have been more so, sitting down in all this after dark.' The hands on her shoulders tightened, and a harshness came into his voice. 'Haven't you any sense?'

She remained static, silent, feeling a rush of love for him well inside her, creating a longing to turn outright into his arms, but she only looked out across the swiftly running water beneath them, and thought: This, too, like that other time in Nerada, I'll remember!

His voice broke the stillness and she felt the feather-light pressure on the top of her head recede a fraction. 'Tell me, Deirdre,' he said, 'tell me, do you like this place?'

'You mean here, Blair, on the river, or Limberg?'

'Actually, I meant here, but you can take my words to cover the larger question. I'd like information on that point too.'

She replied immediately, 'I like it very much, to both questions. I know it's quiet, no city rush and bustle, but I've been made so welcome, and everyone has been more than kind.' If there was a private reservation, she thrust it resolutely into the background of her thoughts.

He appeared satisfied as he carried it no further. They stood so for a moment of time, then with a sighing breath his hands slipped from her shoulder.

'I suppose we'd better return. They'll be sending out a search party soon if you don't make an appearance. Mrs. Liddle would guess where you were when she realizes you're not in the house. Not much misses her eyes, though occasionally some little thing gets by her.' He chuckled, and Deirdre, who by now knew every nuance in his tone, thought he must be wearing what Tony called 'his wicked grin' and wondered fleetingly what mischief he had in mind, or more nearly, what it was that he knew that he was very certain Mrs. Liddle did not.

One hand stayed at her elbow; she felt the presence of his body at her back depart, and he swung her round to face the incline, holding and guiding her along it. She walked obediently beside him, hating to have this so precious brief time with him slip past. Nevertheless, it was vanishing rapidly, as they were now on the path and walking towards the house. Still Blair made no effort to hurry. If anything he was sauntering.

They were nearing the quarters when he spoke from out of the darkness. 'Let's see, Deirdre, you finish here in just over a week, don't you?'

Too miserable at the thought to answer outright, she merely nodded, not caring that he would be unable to see.

The voice continued, level, businesslike, unconcerned, she thought, suddenly angry. 'And you have two small farms to do after that,' he added. 'Maybe five weeks between the two of them all told. That's so, isn't it?'

This time she did answer, surprise in her voice at his knowledge. 'Yes, that's right. My time up here is going swiftly. It seems I've been here a lifetime, though.'

'Not too long a lifetime, I hope.' If she had spoken softly, he for once had not. He appeared gay, cheerful, and she wished she could hate him for his blithe insouciance.

Tentatively she placed her foot on the lower step of the verandah as they stopped at the house, expecting him to say good night and leave. But he walked up the steps beside her, saying, 'I'll come in for a few minutes, Deirdre. I want to speak to Mrs. Liddle.'

Her surprise was obvious. For the whole duration of her stay at the farm he had never once come to their quarters. Actually, he had not even had a conversation with any one of them, merely a smile if he happened to pass by. She pushed open the door of the living-room and stood framed in the aperture, Blair towering behind her.

Norma was in a chair doing embroidery, Marge spread out on her tummy on the floor reading a lurid-covered love story; and both Mrs. Liddle and Edna were at the table writing letters. All eyes came up as Deirdre continued to stand there, then surprise took the place of inquiry. Marge scrambled into a more dignified position, Norma's fancy-work fell unheeded to her lap, and Mrs. Liddle voiced what the rest only showed.

'Blair, what are you doing here? Is something wrong?'

For a brief second his teeth flashed white against the surrounding bronze of his face, one eyebrow quirked incredibly high, but he was serious again as he asked her in formal tones, 'May I come in for a moment? I want to consult you about an outing I had in mind. But first I must tell you; I've just been reading the riot act to young Deirdre here. Didn't you warn her never to sit in the grass after dark? I found her on the bank, dreaming and admiring the river, right bang in the middle of the escarpment among the undergrowth. It was nothing in her young life, having to think of such mundane things as snakes, when she could satisfy her senses with views and scenery. It leads me to think that we've been a little negligent with her welfare.'

The older woman, however, was not smiling with him. She had turned shocked eyes upon Deirdre.

'Heavens, Deirdre, that was a thing so elementary it wouldn't have occurred to me to mention it.' Her gaze swung back to the figure lounging just inside the door. 'I did have your man Richard on the river bank for the first couple of weeks we were here, to keep an eye on them when swimming.'

He only nodded, as he took in Deirdre's startled face.

'He wasn't in evidence, Deirdre,' he explained as if to a child. 'You would never have seen him unless you found yourself in difficulties. Then you would have felt him.'

As her glance swung two and fro, inquiring, and yes, resentful, his voice changed from the friendly note it had held all evening and took on one so often used to her.

'You didn't imagine we would allow you to swim indiscriminately in any part of these waters without supervision, did you? You were hardly of Olympic standard. Still, I must admit you've improved.'

Her voice wrathful at his mocking tone, she turned on him. 'How would you know? I haven't even caught a glimpse of you except out in the paddocks. Certainly not down by the river. And Richard? Why, I've never seen him near us, he's so shy.'

'I would know. I think I've already mentioned that this is my farm and I certainly know what occurs on it . . . on all of it!'

She shrugged, deliberately turning her back.

Mrs. Liddle's voice broke the ensuing silence. 'What was it you wanted to see me about, Blair?'

Leaning against the doorpost, he extracted a cigarette, and went through the familiar routine of lighting it. Exhaling smoke in a long stream, he spoke slowly as if choosing his words. 'I have to go up to Tinaroo this Sunday to see a chap on business. I thought,' he paused to draw on his cigarette, 'I thought we might make a day of it; a bonus for good work, you could call it.' He grinned at the faces turned to him. 'Deirdre was telling me she hadn't seen the dam. As she'll finish grading soon, I suggested she might like to have a look at it.'

'Oh, Mrs. Liddle,' Marge, as usual, when any kind of entertainment was mooted, was all for it. 'It would be scrumptious! Do say yes!'

Deirdre had looked with incredulous eyes in the direction of the doorway. But the eyes that met hers were bland and smug. She could read the challenge of them, daring her to say that she had never mentioned Tinaroo, that she didn't even know where it was.

'Why, I don't know, Blair.' Mrs. Liddle was regretful. 'I couldn't go myself. I have another engagement, and the youngsters by themselves could be a nuisance. Can you make it some other time before we go?' She looked from the hopeful intent faces – even Norma's – of her charges, to the deliberately unhelpful one of that lounging figure in the doorway. After a silence which was not taken advantage of, she went on slowly, 'Perhaps Deirdre would like to go. She really shouldn't miss it while she's up here. Yes . . . yes, all right; if they won't be too much bother on their own. Only look after them.' She glanced at him. 'But I needn't tell you that, need I?'

His answer was as soft as Deirdre had ever heard him speak. 'No, dear Mrs. Liddle, I don't think you do need to.'

Straightening from his slouching position, he faced the darkness outside. 'I think that will be all for now. We can go into it later on. Good night.'

For a wonder it was Deirdre who kept them waiting the following Sunday morning. Nothing would go right. She seemed to have ten thumbs instead of only two, and some fingers. Marge, ready and impatient on the verandah, kept up a running commentary on her tardiness. Deirdre heard the sound of Mrs. Liddle's voice, and smiled to herself as Marge became silent. Their mentor certainly managed them all! There was a murmur of sound from outside, the faintest swish of tyres, and she knew that the car had arrived. Giving her hair a final pat, she caught up her gauze scarf and her beach bag of odds and ends, then, automatically drawing the deep breath she found needful whenever meeting Blair, she walked on to the verandah.

Waiting at the bottom of the steps, its paintwork scintillating in the bright sunshine as though it had just been freshly washed and polished, the car stood with both doors open. Marge waited beside it, exasperation plainly written on her face at this, to her, uncalled-for delay.

Blair, sitting sideways on the railway talking to Mrs. Liddle, slid down as Deirdre appeared. He walked across, reached for her bag. 'Ready?' he smiled, a perfectly normal friendly smile, and stood back to allow her to precede him. As she made for the back door of the car, his hand came under her elbow and she was firmly propelled into the front seat. Slipping inside, she looked quickly up at him. He grinned down at her, unashamedly enjoying himself, and dangled her bag from one finger.

'Move up a little, Deirdre.' He slid the container along the seat as she did so. 'Phil has to fit in there too.'

Averting her eyes, she moved further towards the centre of the car. He seated the others, then slipped behind the wheel. A casual wave of the hand to their mentor and the big vehicle was eased forward.

Deirdre would have liked to ask why Phil couldn't sit in the back with Marge, but she didn't care to ask questions and be on the receiving end of the sort of answer she might get. Marge too would have liked to inquire about the same thing, but she was wary of Blair as she was of no one else.

The answer to both of them was soon forthcoming. The car pulled in towards the hotel opposite two figures waiting under the verandah. Deirdre glanced quickly back at Norma, then at the form beside her, whose smile was quizzical as he met her look.

'Isn't this what you wanted, Deirdre?' he questioned softly, as Phil slid in next to her and Tony opened the back door.

The car was moving again, really fast now. Phil had turned to slide his arm across the backrest to enable him to see Marge while he talked to her, squashing Deirdre further against the figure lounging, she thought, too indolently behind the wheel of such a powerful vehicle.

She heard a low chuckle, and a voice equally low saying, 'There must be something about you, Deirdre. Certainly, I've never intervened in a love affair before . . . except my own, of course.' The low voice held a mocking inflection as it gave this information. 'However, I imagine my including Tony today pleases you. Heaven send that, in my first attempt at match-making, I won't live to regret it.' His voice sobered. 'I only wish I could interfere in Bill Darrell's.'

Deirdre looked her surprise. He wasn't amused or even thinking of her. His gaze, sombre and cold, was fixed on the road unfolding before them. Her words came involuntarily. 'I would expect you to dare anything if it suited you, Blair.'

'I would if I knew or even thought that I was right, Deirdre,' his reply was careful, considered. 'But with Bill's affairs, I just don't know.' Then deliberately, he shrugged. 'Well, as yet, there's nothing to be done about that, however,' his gaze went to the rear vision mirror. 'Let's see how my first attempt is going,' he was smiling again.

She couldn't help but ask, 'You're not worried about them, then, Blair?'

His glance slid sideways. 'Of course I'm not. I wouldn't have arranged it, if I had been,' he answered. 'Tony knows exactly why I asked him. He could quite easily have been too busy to come. He knew who would be making up the party, and also, you know, he does know what he's doing, even if you in your wide experience think that he might not.'

'Oh.'

'What's the "Oh" for, Deirdre? Don't you think you have a wide experience?' His voice was even lower than before, as he went on, only just audible above the rush of wind and the murmur of the engine – certainly unable to be heard by the others, who were listening with varying degrees of belief to a tall story Phil was expounding. 'What do you say to burying the hatchet, baby? Just relax and enjoy yourself for today.'

She ventured no reply and slipped down deep into her seat, gazing unhappily through the windscreen, profoundly conscious of his presence at her side. Nevertheless, her thoughts did swing to Bill. She had not connected him with an unhappy love-affair. To her, he was attractive, charming, full of warmth, a man any girl would be proud to have in love with her. Honesty compelled her to admit that this, the man at her side, was not. He was too arrogant, too self-sufficient, too determined to have his own way regardless ... aided certainly by the confident assumption that his way was the right way.

Her eyes followed the line of the long polished bonnet to pause at the leaping jungle figure crouched at its extreme edge, and she knew that whenever she saw one of these cars with the flying silver jaguar, her mind would jump instantly to this man leaning so indolently at her side. Somehow in all the months up here, Blair and his car had become synonymous, perhaps because in a community such as this, with its empty distant spaces, a car was as much a part of living as was a home. An exclamation from Marge of 'Oh, goody, fish and chips! Don't they smell scrumptious?' brought her attention back to the present.

She could see they were travelling through a town which she surmised must be Atherton, and there certainly was a delectable odour of frying fish. Marge had said no more, but hoped the implication would do its work.

The form beside Deirdre moved, as Blair turned and exclaimed over his shoulder, 'You young Philistine, Marge! Of course you're not going to have fish and chips. I've packed a hamper which I hope is much more to our taste, and also, I hope too, much better for our digestion.'

Marge subsided without a word. Phil gave a quiet chuckle, and there was silence in the car.

Gazing back the way they had come, over hundreds of miles of cultivated farmlands, bush and mountains, Deirdre saw a spiral of smoke rising lazily skywards in the far distance, much as if one had laid down a half-smoked cigarette on to an ashtray. She guessed that way out there a bush fire must be burning, but from this vantage point it was only one more addition to the beauty of a scenic view.

'You'll be seeing the lake in a minute, Deirdre,'

Norma remarked, leaning forward to gaze ahead. 'It stretches for miles where once it was only bushlands and forests.'

And it did indeed stretch for miles. The great expanse of water was like a huge inland sea. Deirdre gazed at it, fascinated as they drove parallel along its restless length and mounted a small hill to stop directly across from a landscaped pavilion.

Blair cut the engine, turned slightly to face all five. 'Well, here we are.' One eyebrow rose. 'Any suggestions?' His glance was bland as he looked at Tony, who, however, only answered mildly, 'I would like to walk across the dam if you don't mind, Blair. I would like to see how much more water has piled up since I was last here. It's of interest to us, you know, seeing that the project is for our tobacco.'

Deirdre thought to herself that he could hold his own with Blair's mockery, even if he was the type of man with not a lot to say. They walked through the pavilion which commemorated the building of the vast project, out on to the great cement walk. It was huge, and had a severe constructional elegance that impressed her, but she admitted silently to herself that it could be oppressive, and yes, a little frightening too. The dammed water spread far into the distance; not a gentle and placid sheet of water this; it appeared to have a life of its own with little angry waves slapping against the concrete barrier which held it confined. She reflected with a shiver that it

166

must be very deep, compared to its opposing side which could be seen dropping endlessly from a dizzy height.

In the middle of the walk she gazed with awe over the giant spillway, very glad for more than one reason of the presence by her side, the hand firm on her elbow, which despite all reason spelt safety, complete protection. Watching the water gushing forth in a curtain of iridescent spray as it began its immense fall to the bottom, she was reminded of the coloured soap bubbles on the plates that first day she had washed up on Blair's farm. She wondered, sadly, if all her life through things that happened would abruptly bring his face before her mind's eye.

She gave a tiny sigh of relief when they decided to leave. The wide walk was crammed with people, tourists from all over Australia, the foreign number-plates on their cars being more plentiful than the home-grown variety; youngsters up for the water sports, and of course, families out for a day's picnic. The noise was bedlam, as mere humans tried to out-vie the clamour of wind and water. Norma and Tony had disappeared in the crush, Marge and Phil were just ahead. But she was happy, content to keep her arm loose by her side, the hand holding it guiding her firmly through the throng ... content enough for this day that he had told her to relax and enjoy; to care only that he was there beside her and think of no future beyond it.

The others were waiting for them as they stepped off the walk, and they sauntered, in no hurry, through the sparkling day. A lovely day, Deirdre gave thanks, although up here most days were lovely. Still, it could have been grey and rainy; she shook off the depressing thought as they came to their own particular parking spot and grinned as Marge said to no one in particular that she was hungry, weren't they ever going to have lunch?

'We'll have it right now, if you're actually starving,' Blair told her, and added: 'I wouldn't care to have that on my conscience to face Mrs. Liddle with!'

He unlocked the boot, withdrawing among other objects a folding table and three camp stools. Phil took hold of them, setting the table in the shade of a tree and bowing the three girls on to the small seats.

There was nothing fumbling or inefficient about these men. Apparently they could look after themselves . . . and anyone else, too, in the food line, as well as farm tobacco. They went to work in the capacious luggage compartments of the car and the meal was handed over with a flourish in no time at all. And it was an inducement to the eye as well as to the gastric juices. Arranged among salad vegetables, red, green, yellow, silver-white, was delicious-looking chicken, fried brown and crisp, and around one side, vying with their colours for notice, succulent pink ham added its own enticement.

Phil took his lunch and sat on the grass cross-legged before them. Tony dropped down by Norma's chair, and Deirdre, who had a normal girl's healthy appetite at the sight of such tempting food, found that all at once it had deserted her. Blair had walked across, plate in hand, and seated himself, not like Tony at a discreet distance, but directly along-side her stool, his shoulders practically against her knees, his head level with her arm. He began to eat, unconcernedly joining in the conversation, while she remained frozen, a chicken leg held in one hand, looking down at the head below her.

She had never before seen it at this angle, and the brown face under the glinting silver hair seemed foreshortened and strange. It was not unusual to be unable to see his eyes wide open, but lashes she had never noticed fanned the lean tanned cheeks as he gazed downwards at his plate. Unexpectedly they flew up, and the eyes they sheltered looked directly into hers.

Flushing, dazed a little, she averted her own too revealing look and bent low over her lunch, waiting for the inevitable remarks. None came. Blair was eating some salad, his attention entirely given to it, his head downbent again. This time her glance did not linger on him, and raising her chicken to her mouth, she began slowly to eat.

There was no comment on her half-eaten lunch, as she was handed in exchange her fruit salad re-posing in its outer dish of crushed ice, and she heard without surprise his announcement immediately he had finished that he would get along to his business appointment. Could they amuse themselves for an hour or so? Not waiting for an acknowledgement he indicated the big picnic hamper, and with a glance from the two men to the soiled dishes remarked with a grin, 'It's all yours!'

Deirdre helped stack dishes away and tidy up, her mind on anything but what she was doing, registering only that appalling moment of a short time ago, wondering if he had read in her expression what must have been so apparent in that split instant of exposure. Indignation came to her rescue; she reflected sharply that it was just like him. No other man would so unexpectedly look up and away as he had done when he should have been concentrating solely on his food.

Finished, she went to sit on the rug that Phil had so carefully placed on the shady side of the car, pushing a cushion comfortably behind her shoulders. She closed her eyes and leant back, content to follow any plans the others decided upon. The breeze off the lake played upon her shut lids and gradually her head eased down to lie upon the pillow, the sounds of a busy picnic ground receding from her consciousness.

She woke abruptly with a feeling of urgency, then smiled at her alarm. Two car loads of youngsters had pulled in beside them, going about their unloading of water-skis and other impedimenta with the noise and unconcern teenagers invariably accord their surroundings the world over. Blair was at the far end of the rug, leaning back against the car, reading, one hand resting negligently over a bent knee, a cigarette dangling from his fingers. Of the rest of the party there was no sign. Knowing she must look dishevelled and half dazed still from sleep, she glanced at him thinking crossly that he would be there to see her like this; not realizing that her flushed face and disordered hair lent her a charm of innocence freshly awakened.

'Would you care for a cup of tea, Deirdre?'

He was regarding her impersonally from across the distance separating them, and to anyone not conversant with him, he appeared pleasant, normal. Nevertheless, she could see that the tiny lines about his mouth were more than usually indented, and unguarded, his eyes showed a tiredness which was entirely foreign. Suddenly her heart went out to him in an upsurge of warmth and love, wishing that she could smooth away the lines and see him laugh – even if it were only to mock at her. In her most private thoughts laughter and Blair went together, and she wondered suddenly if his business appointment had caused him worry.

'Have you got to consider it so seriously, Deirdre? I myself could drink half a dozen cups. Everything is prepared except for the adding of tea-leaves.' Her eyes followed his gesture to a brick fireplace further down the slope, which she could see held more than one billy across the blackened fire-bar. Suspended above flames that showed only a pale semblance of their night-time brilliance in having to compete with blazing sunshine, they had issuing forth a faint cloud of vapour to show that they were already on the boil.

About to decline as he made a movement to rise, the words faltered on her lips. He was smiling now, a real smile, the knowledge of what she was about to do making the blue eyes glint. She raised her head higher, saying primly instead, 'Yes, thank you, Blair, I would love a cup of tea.'

She received her reward; her wish of only a moment ago. He was openly laughing at her as he said, 'O.K. Don't move. I'll make the tea. The others can be lucky enough to return now, or brew their own when they come back.'

She found her beach bag, used her lipstick and comb, hastily finishing as he arrived back, a billy full of scalding tea in one hand.

A cloth appeared in the centre of the rug between them, a rich mouth-watering chocolate cake adorning it. He answered with a nod her look of recognition.

'Yes, Mrs. Turley's. She tells me it's a favourite with all you girls.' Tiny sandwiches and savoury biscuits came from the car as he was talking.

Taking the cup of hot strong tea he handed her, she inquired with a shake of her head, 'Truly, Blair, is there anything you don't know?' and was taken aback when he answered her idle question seriously.

'Not very much where it concerns me, I should imagine!'

He placed sandwiches and biscuits on a plate and passed it across, then started in on the cake.

Deirdre protested, laughing, but none the less inclined to mean it. 'No, really, Blair. I'll get as fat as I don't know what, if I eat all that. You're as bad as Mrs. Liddle. She's always trying to fatten me up. It's not very complimentary.'

'I shouldn't think that Mrs. Liddle had any intention of being complimentary,' he retorted dryly. And knowing that same lady, Deirdre thought that this would indeed be so.

'She realizes you work hard – well, not hard, but consistently,' Blair continued, 'and doubtless feels you should eat plenty too. You do understand, don't you, that you look a different girl from the one who came to us?' His voice changed. 'Does she still make you drink your milk, Deirdre?'

'Don't tell me you know about that too, Blair? That *is* the limit! I'm not a baby.'

'Aren't you indeed!' Matter-of-fact, the question came.

She spun quickly away from that subject to the safety of Mrs. Liddle.

'Why, even Marge feels sorry for me, saying "Poor Deirdre" every time I have to force that great glass of milk down at every meal. I expect you know that it's not only at your farm but all the places we've been to. I like milk,' she continued a little heatedly, 'but sometimes I may not feel like it, and I contend that I'm old enough to say no if I want to.'

'And do you say no?' mildly.

Deirdre laughed at that and shrugged. 'Really, Blair, you should know Mrs. Liddle better than that! Of course I don't. It wouldn't do me any good if I did.'

'But then I expect I know her from a different angle from you, Deirdre. I'm not in the category of having to drink milk.'

Reluctantly she smiled, her mood still one of indignation at her remembered wrongs.

'I wish you were,' her tone was heartfelt. 'I would just love to see you made to do something you didn't want to do.' As the enormity of her words penetrated her consciousness, a hand flew to her mouth. Horrified, her eyes gazed at him. But his, bluer than the seas at home in deep summer, showed only amusement.

'And for that, Deirdre,' he gave answer, 'you might live to see the day. We'll have to wait and see, won't we?'

She turned, glad to abandon the subject, as the absent ones returned. They were listening perforce to Marge, who on observing Deirdre watching her, said bitterly:

'Oh, Deirdre, I met Steven Case over at the lake.

He has his speed-boat here, and offered to let me try out on his water-skis, but Norma said no. It's not fair!'

'I didn't say no, Deirdre,' Norma cut in quietly, distressed. 'I said go and ask Blair. You can imagine what Mrs. Liddle would say if anything went wrong.' There was a small silence. They could indeed imagine.

'It seems, Marge, that once again I'm the dragon where you're concerned, because the answer is definitely no. Apart from the possibility of an accident, I think,' glancing at his wrist-watch, 'we shall only have time to finish our tea. It's a long drive home.'

Norma's face showed her relief as she dropped down beside Deirdre to accept the cup of tea Blair was handing to her.

CHAPTER TEN

A BOOK in her lap, Deidre sat in the lamplit room; her head might have been sedulously bent over it, but she had turned no page in the last fifteen minutes. This was their last farm, she was thinking disconsolately, and only a small one at that. Her eyes fixed unseeingly on the print before her, she wondered if she would see Blair again before they left in three days' time. He had moved them, when they had finished his grading, and Mrs. Liddle's truck in the garage for an overhaul was not yet ready. Solicitously he had seen that they had every help, even going so far as to see that they were properly ensconced in their new quarters; and she had seen him only once since, in town a fortnight ago.

She sat, remembering with nostalgia the journey home from Tinaroo. Curled up between the two men, she had sat silent, listening happily to the singing that Marge had started; and had known that now, this very moment, was the sum of all aspiration for her. Marge had a good party voice, Norma's and Blair's helped swell the volume, Phil sang quite well. But Tony . . . she wondered why she had never before heard him sing, and then reflected that she had not ever been to his own farm, to his parties where he probably did perform. They were entering the familiar road to home when Norma spoke softly to him. His voice took up the refrain of 'When you come to the end of a perfect day'. She had sat spellbound. The last notes died away into silence. No one made any attempt to sing again, and she thought that for her, too, it had been a perfect day; that even if one's heart's desire was unobtainable, it was still a good world when sun-drenched days such as this could be remembered.

She raised her head suddenly, listening. She had caught the sound of a car engine coming down the track. It was too silent to belong to a truck, and Stan had collected Edna earlier. She tensed, then relaxed deliberately, scolding herself for being foolish. A car door slammed, and footsteps came swiftly towards their quarters. When Blair stood in the doorway, it was as if a gale of wind had swirled suddenly into the little room. Deirdre always connected him with laughter and exuberance, but tonight he imparted an aura of ... she tried to pin it down, but could find no comparison. His eyes glittered blue and challenging from an ultra-sunburnt face and Mrs. Liddle must have received a like impression. She asked him without a greeting, 'You look as if you've won the lottery, Blair. Have you?'

The lids came swiftly down, and through hooded eyes he scrutinized the room, saying only, 'I haven't heard as much yet, but there's always hope. We've had a good tobacco sale, however, as I expect you already know. You generally manage to keep an eye on things.'

Was there mockery in that voice? Deirdre couldn't be sure.

He continued, speaking to Mrs. Liddle, 'I've come to take Deirdre to a tennis meeting. I imagine, as they think this may be her last week here, they want to present her with a little memento of Limberg.'

'Why, Blair, how nice!' There was genuine warmth in the older woman's voice. She turned to Deirdre and told her, 'Run along and get ready, Blair won't mind waiting a minute. You've already showered.'

Deirdre returned in just about that amount of time, clad in lemon pleated cotton, her face repowdered, her hair swinging free and shining from its hasty brushing. Blair stood aside from the door, then followed close behind her.

Silent in her place by the car window, a bare foot of space separating them, she watched as he lit a cigarette. There was no glance at her tonight as he used the dashboard lighter; his attention was concentrated solely on the road, on the ribbon unfolding before him in the blazing headlights. It was a mere matter of minutes before they were running into the small town, and, she noticed with surprise, going straight through and out the other side. Speaking for the first time, she inquired, 'Where's the meeting to be held, Blair?'

'We're not going to any meeting. I want to talk to

you and I didn't fancy going in there and saying, "Come along, Deirdre, I'm taking you out." If I had to,' he shrugged, 'I would. For the present : . .'

She blankly took in the shrug and the unfinished sentence, wondering what in the name of heaven he could want to speak with her about. She gazed out of the window beside her, hardly taking in the familiar outline of trees and farms as they rushed towards them and away again, in a shadowy night lit only by starshine. She did see that, unexpectedly, they were on the road that led to Blair's own farm. Without a word he got out and opened the gate when they arrived there, returned and drove the car through, then sent it skimming down the avenue. She noted, even at such a time, that he had not bothered to get out of the car to re-close the barred entrance. It brought to mind the very first occasion that she had come here, when it was Edna who had jumped down to open it, and that while waiting for her to return, Mrs. Liddle had sat in the high cabin of her truck talking about the farm as it had been in the old days when Blair's mother and father had been alive. It had been Deirdre's first glimpse of Blair's domestic background to compare with the one she had of him as a white-clad figure flashing back and forth on a tennis court, looking glamorous in such different clothes from every other player — from the one leaning so indolently behind the wheel of his car; or, more close to her heart, being held in his arms on a dance floor. Well, she could smell his mother's oleanders now; their perfume was all about her, but she spared no thought for them at all as she watched that shadowy woman's son cut the engine and switch off the headlights, leaving only the dashboard glow for illumination. He slid an arm along the backrest and looked directly at her across the intervening space.

'Well, Deirdre,' the words were quietly spoken, but she could sense another tone underlying the softness, 'what do I do? Kiss you first and talk afterwards, or talk first and kiss you later?'

She turned, fumbling for the door handle. But she was stopped and pulled firmly back, his arms around her, cradling her head to his shoulder.

'Don't be silly, Deirdre! This time – despite what you may have heard to the contrary – my intentions are strictly honourable. I may not have had a lot of rehearsal for this kind of thing, but I expect I had to come to it some time. It seems that that time is here and now. Wouldn't you really like to marry me?'

When the meaning of what he had actually said penetrated, indignation was the uppermost emotion in her mind. It gave to her the necessary impetus to sit upright and face him.

But he said again softly, glinting his smile at her, 'Don't you want to marry me, my darling?' The last two words did it.

'You can't be serious, Blair? Why, this isn't how one asks someone to marry them!'

'No, Deirdre? Tell me how it's done, and I'll try to rectify any omission.'

She could only gaze at him speechlessly.

'Enough of this. Come here.'

She was drawn back, close, into his arms; her head again on his shoulder, hair falling everywhere. He stroked the shining strands gently back from her temples, his fingers following the taut-drawn line downwards, finding her chin, tilting it towards him. His face came close, closer, disintregrating the silhouette which the star-studded sky behind had made of him. But the lips that found hers were not gentle; they demanded ... and she was pulled even more tightly into those unyielding arms, surrendering herself, too, unreservedly into that embrace for which she had so longed.

Then those lips lifted, slowly, reluctantly, and it was Blair, this time, who drew the deep-drawn breath as he put her, none too gently, from his arms 'There you are. I hope you're satisfied.' The words too were not gentle, they were clipped, curt. 'Do you think I haven't wanted to do that all these weeks, knowing you were just up the path a few yards, sleeping in the old house? Well! I'll expect some recompense for the self-denial I've had to practise. I'm just not made to meander through a conventional engagement, Deirdre, and although I knew after that episode by Henry's car that you were not entirely indifferent to me, I couldn't say, "Marry me now, Deirdre", and take you from Mrs.

Liddle when she was straining every nerve to meet her commitments. Now could I? My beloved reason for existing!' His fingers traced the outline of her face and drifted to rest in the hollow of her throat. His voice stopped and his lips resting on her forehead travelled slowly downwards. She sat immobile, transfixed, waiting for them to continue, but they remained stationary beside her mouth. His words came muffled. 'Do you know that poor Charles nearly got his head knocked off the day you first played tennis here? I'd never before experienced anything in my life like the feeling that gripped me when I saw him standing there with his arm about you. I knew in that moment that my whole way of life was finished, changed; and I wasn't at all sure that I wanted it changed, but. . . .' The lips moved a fraction, and she was caught up again in timelessness, ecstasy.

Once again it was he who drew away, and spoke in a tone he strove to make level, calm. 'I've made arrangements for Mr. Henderson to marry us in a couple of weeks, Deirdre. You can go to Cairns and get your trousseau in that time, can't you? Actually, I've booked two Saturday afternoons, but I give you fair warning that I'm not the most patient of men, and the furthest away is a damned long time off.'

As the import of these words came through the mist of rapture surrounding her, Deirdre came upright for the second time and stared at him. 'Blair, you haven't!' she ejaculated. 'Not even you could go about things in such a high-handed manner! And who ... who ...' her voice rose, 'is Mr. Henderson?'

Calmly he answered, 'Didn't you know? He's the minister from the church you attended in Nerada. I hoped very much that you wouldn't want to be married in Cairns. I thought that you, my docile little lamb, wouldn't want to upset arrangements already made.' There was a glimpse of the Blair she was more accustomed to than the one holding her now, the Blair she loved. 'Also, Deirdre,' he went on, 'all my friends are up here. I simply couldn't let them miss my wedding. They'll all be so delighted that I'm caught at last.'

She ignored this side-tracking, but pulled back into his embrace again, all objections went with the wind; and she knew that whatever arrangements he had made would be the ones she would want. A smile curved her lips as she said with illusory humility:

'Very well, anything you say, Blair.'

The form holding her so close began to shake. His words when they came still contained an element of laughter. 'Yes, I'll bet, my beloved! Your behaviour up to now certainly points that way. We'll see, though. Do I take it that your answer is for Saturday week?' He lifted her face with one finger as she remained silent, obviously reading his answer there, once more his mouth rested on hers for an aeon of eternity. Straightening up, he told her reluctantly,

'I'd better take you home, my darling, and get down to actual arrangements.'

'Oh, Blair!' At the horror in her tone, he swung back quickly. 'Now what?'

'Mrs. Liddle and the girls. Whatever will I say to them?'

His hand had gone back to his jacket pocket hanging over the seat. He said carelessly, 'I suppose you really don't have to say very much. Just hold out your hand with this on it and say casually, "Look, I'm engaged."' He had possessed himself of her hand and she felt the ring slip on to her finger.

'There you are. It's been burning a hole in my dressing-table drawer for nearly two months. Two of the longest months of my life, I'll have you know. They just wouldn't pass.'

'Do you mean to tell me, Blair, that you bought this ring for me two whole months ago and said nothing?' she demanded incredulously. 'Not only said nothing, but behaved often as if I didn't exist, especially when I was working here. I was so unhappy at the time,' she recalled, 'that I didn't know how I was going to face the future.'

That certainly gratified him.

'Without me?' he demanded. 'But the truth is I acted, rightly or wrongly, for what I believed to be the best.'

She gazed at him ruefully through the starshine.

'But what will Mrs. Liddle say?' she asked, fluttering her hands protestingly. 'It may well be all right for you to be so casual, Blair, but they'll all be so amazed about this. No one can possibly have believed that you were serious about me.'

'Oh, yes, Deirdre, two people were well aware of it. And since yesterday there are three. I told Lexia what my intentions were, and she's planning a trip overseas. I suppose you could say that we have her blessing, but you don't have to if you don't want to.'

Deirdre sat silent, thinking of Lexia, so beautiful, and so much more suited to Blair than she was. Why, the two would complement one another. She wondered when Lexia's journey had been planned, before or after Blair outlined to her his future plans, and she felt reasonably certain that it was after. But, Blair being Blair, she would never know.

His voice continued: 'And of course Bill knows. He's always known, right from the first day when I took you to lunch after meeting you off the train. I'm not in the habit of lending support to lonely young girls I run into at railway stations. And Tony must have guessed, even if he isn't completely sure. It's a wonder the whole town doesn't know, the way I've been feeling lately. As for Mrs. Liddle, would you like to wait until tomorrow to tell her, and I'll come over after breakfast and lend my support?'

But she clung to him suddenly, and very shyly, eager all at once that all the world should know of her sudden bewildering happiness.

'No, Blair, let's tell her tonight. ... After all, it's only fair, and she's been good to me.'

'She certainly has. I saw to that.' He kissed her hair again, lightly, a butterfly touch. 'I'd like to ask you in and show you over the house – your house very soon now! But I think on the whole it will be wiser to let that wait and take you straight back to Mrs. Liddle.' He grinned at her one-sidedly, his blue eyes curiously brilliant. 'I know my own weaknesses, my pet, and – anyway we'll be married so soon! I certainly shall see to that!'